Unconsenting Adults

TRISHNA CHAUDHURI

Copyright © 2025 by Trishna Chaudhuri

All rights reserved.

This book or any portion thereof may not be reproduced or used in any manner whatsoever without the express written permission of the respective writer of the respective content except for the use of brief quotations in a book review.

The writer of the respective work holds sole responsibility for the originality of the content and IndiePress is not responsible in any way whatsoever.

Printed in India

ISBN: 978-93-7197-099-0

First Printing, 2025

IndiePress

A division of Nasadiya Technologies Private Ltd.

Koramangala, Bengaluru

Karnataka-560029

http://indiepress.in/

Edited by MAP Systems, Bengaluru

Typeset by MAP Systems, Bengaluru

Book Cover designed by Sankhasubhro Nath

Publishing Consultant: Shrey Saboo

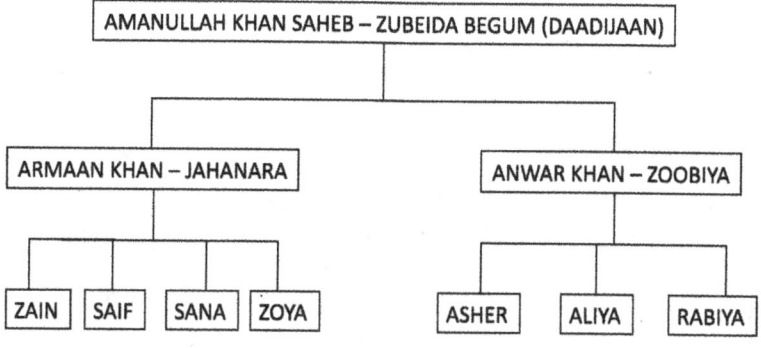

[1]

'I can't believe it, Ashar. How did you agree to this?' mocked Zain, cradling the phone against his shoulder as he shaved.

'Don't even ask, *bhai*. It all happened so quickly that I had no choice,' replied Ashar. 'Though frankly, I think I got lucky.'

'Lucky!' said Zain, switching on the speaker on his phone as he continued to shave.

'Yes, Zain. I know it is an arranged marriage and all that, but Saniya is quite lovely, full of life, and Walid Uncle and his family have become quite close to Mom and Dad. Walid Uncle and Dad were in school and college together.'

'But how do you know you are lucky, Ashar? You don't even know Saniya. How could you agree to this? Who has an arranged marriage in this day and age? I heard that they had already fixed everything even before you met Saniya. I am sure *Daadijaan* had a hand in this.'

'Ha ha. Very true! She was visiting Walid Uncle with Mom and Dad, and I suddenly got a call from *Daadijaan* while I was at work. She just said, "I am sending you my location, I want you here tomorrow," and disconnected the phone. After that, she wouldn't answer any of my calls, and neither did

Mom or Dad. So, I panicked, rushed home, bundled Rabiya and Aliya into the car, and drove all the way to Dehradun.'

'Ouch! That must have been quite an eventful drive. The girls must have eaten your head!'

'Ha ha. Yes, they did, but I was so worried. I didn't care.'

'Once we reached, I found *Daadijaan* sitting there like a queen holding on to a girl's hand. She said, "Meet your bride."'

'Good Lord! *Daadijaan* is such a drama queen, she really should have joined Hindi films. Sometimes, I really think she missed her true calling. But, still, I cannot believe you agreed, Ashar. I would never have...'

'Try saying no to *Daadijaan*... Don't worry, *bhai*, your time will also come...'

'Never...'

'Anyway, the wedding is in two weeks and *Daadijaan* has already called Uncle, and you all have to be here by Sunday, so you can sleep off your jetlag and stuff, and join the wedding celebrations. Everything will be in Dehradun. Destination wedding – ha ha ha!'

'We will be there, we won't miss it. I still cannot believe you agreed to this,' said Zain, signing off.

Later in the evening, Zain, chatting with his mom on the phone said, '*Ammi*, tell *Baba* that our tickets are done for India, we leave on Friday night and should be there by Saturday night. I've already told Saif and the girls. It is a hopping flight via London, so I will join you all in London and we can then fly together. I am going to be in London on work anyway.'

'Zain, yes, I will tell him. The next few days are going to be crazy! Going to India on such short notice, and that too for a wedding! I think I will go crazy shopping over the next few days. But, honestly, your *Daadijaan* takes the cake! She called me and said, "Jahaanara, get on the next flight and don't bother with clothes. We will have everything organised here." She is still such a Hitler, I cannot believe Anwar *bhai* and Zoobiya agreed to this alliance, so what if the girl is Anwar *bhai*'s classmate's daughter, they didn't even ask for Ashar's opinion! Did you hear how your *Daadijaan* made Ashar rush to Dehradun? She is really the limit! I cannot believe Ashar agreed as well...'

'*Ammi, Ammi,* I have spoken to Ashar, he told me all about it! What did you expect from your total filmy mother-in-law? *Daadijaan* is a total drama queen! But, honestly, I agree with you... I don't know how Ashar agreed, I would never have. Though, he didn't sound too upset about the whole thing.'

'Zain, what do you mean, you would never have... I would never put you in such a situation! Times have changed; your *Daadijaan* needs to also change...'

'*Ammi,* you and I both know that in front of *Daadijaan*, neither you nor *Chachi,* and for that matter nor do *Baba* and *Chacha,* ever stand a chance... anyway, I am getting into a meeting, I will see you all in London. Bye *Ammi!*'

[2]

'They are here! Seher and Sophia, get the flowers ready, the *baraat* is here! Where is Sara? Uff, that girl will drive me mad... Forget her, all of you get ready!'

Shazia Walid Ali was going crazy. Being the mother of the bride was not easy—and especially not easy to organise at such short notice. There was so much to do, and though there were so many people around, no one seemed to be doing anything. She thought to herself... Saniya's *nikaah* is only the first one. I shall have to do this for the other three girls as well... God help me!

The wedding party was welcomed with flowers and music, and everyone settled into their rooms for the two-day destination wedding at a beautiful old *haveli* (heritage house) at the foothills of the Himalayas.

Daadijaan, the grand old lady and the groom's grandmother, was resting in her room, beaming at everything going on around her. Her grandson, Ashar, was getting married. He would be the first of this generation—though she would have preferred her eldest grandson, Zain to be the first, but well, she was sure that too would happen soon.

She lay back on the bed and sighed to herself when she heard a clicking and tapping sound. Looking around, she couldn't see anyone, but the tapping and clicking continued. Getting off the bed, she walked towards the sound and reached the heavy curtains near the French windows. Yanking them apart, she saw a young girl, busy on her laptop, surrounded by thick books and notes.

'Hello! Who are you?'

Fingers freezing over the keyboard as she was suddenly startled, the girl turned around and saw a beautiful elderly lady peering at her. 'I... I am Sara...'

'Sara...? Saniya's youngest sister?'

'Yes, you must be *Daadijaan*, Saniya *aapi* was talking about you.'

'How come we haven't met you yet? And, what are you doing here, hiding behind my curtains?'

'I study at boarding school and have exams in a week's time. They didn't think about my exams and just made me come home for the wedding... Can you imagine, *Daadijaan*? Who does that? What if I fail? What will people say—Professor Ali's daughter has failed her board exams... I'm so nervous and there is hardly any time!'

'*Daadijaan*, please let me sit here and study. Anyway, they keep forgetting I am there—but if they see me, I keep getting chores, and then I won't be able to study at all!'

Daadijaan couldn't help smiling, hearing the poor girl's helplessness.

'Okay... okay... take a little break and come and have a cup of *chai* with me. I won't tell anyone. Tell me about yourself.'

'About me? *Daadijaan*, I'm very boring. Should I call Seher or Sophia *aapi*? My sisters are much better company.'

'Come, come, dear, you have to taste my *adrak-waali chai*, I carry my own tea leaves and brew my chai myself. You will love it! Come, come, take a half-hour break. You deserve a break from those thick textbooks and that blessed computer!'

Half an hour later:

'There you are, Sara! We were wondering where you were! Sara, *Ammi* wanted you to go and get ready. We were looking for you to wrap some presents but couldn't find you.'

Seher and Sofia, Sara's sisters, entered *Daadijaan*'s room with four other girls their age.

'Hello *Daadijaan*, are you having *chai*?' one of the girls asked, hugging the old lady, 'We came to see if you were okay.'

'Rabiya, Aliya, Sana and Zoya, meet Sara—our youngest sister, the one *Ammi* has been looking for,' Seher said, turning to introduce the girls to Sara.

'*Daadijaan*, you've already met Sara!' Sofia exclaimed.

'Sara has been entertaining me with all her stories about boarding school and how all of you bully her when she is here,' *Daadijaan* laughed and replied.

'Sara, get up and go to *Ammi*—she needs you for something. I think it's to do with looking after some gifts or something,' Seher said, glancing at her and glared. 'Don't listen to her stories, *Daadijaan*! We hardly get to see her when she is here;

she prefers her books and *khaala*'s company in the kitchen to ours!'

Sara looked at *Daadijaan* with a pained expression, then glanced at her books and reluctantly stood up.

'Girls, I want to rest—be off with you all! And let Sara stay—she was massaging my head while we chatted. *Chalo*... off with you all!'

The girls got up to leave, giggling amongst themselves.

Once they had left, *Daadijaan* looked at Sara and told her, 'Go and study. You can go and get ready in an hour.'

Stunned at *Daadijaan*'s kindness, Sara gave her a dazzling smile and rushed to hide behind the curtains again.

Daadijaan closed her eyes as she lay down on the bed, a smile on her face, looking quite angelic. Anyone who knew *Daadijaan* would have known that she was up to something—but there was no one around to catch the expression.

[3]

'Zain! Zain?! Will you stop working—please! My wedding is in a few hours and we have to get ready—and here you are, typing away like a madman! Saif, your brother is a workaholic!' ranted Ashar.

'Ashar *bhai*, please let *bhai* work! If he works, I get to relax and lead a life of leisure. *Baba* has been after my life to join work for the past six months, but I want to chill, travel and fall in love. After I do all that, only then will I join work! I don't want to become like *Bhai*—at such a young age,' said Saif, lounging on the couch against the wall.

'Fall in love!' said Ashar, grinning. 'Wow! That is an interesting list!'

'No list—he has to first get his MBA, and only then will he be allowed to breathe or travel! Till then, neither *Baba* nor I shall sign any cheque,' said Zain without a change in expression or even moving his eyes from his laptop screen.

'Oh god, Zain *Bhai*, please, please give me a break!' pleaded Saif. 'There are so many beautiful girls here! Ashar *Bhai*, your sisters-in-law are all so pretty; you have to introduce me to all of them. I love weddings in India so much colour, such beauty, so much fun.... Our lives in the US are all draped in dull colours—everything is grey and black and more grey. Even *Baba, Ammi* and Sana and Zoya all have become totally American—all very straight, boring, everyone wears beige, grey, black, or white. Everything looks like sephora. Here, in India, it is as though one has stepped into a rainbow all the time! I love it!'

Ashar, quite amused with Saif's monologue, remarked, 'Come on— don't exaggerate! Zain, this guy is hilarious!'

Zain grimaced without a break in his typing.

'Are you asking Zain *bhai?*' retorted Saif. 'He is not even sephora: he is grayscale—everything in his life, his house, his clothes—everything is grey, black, or white, sometimes with a hint of blue. Even the solo orchid on his breakfast counter is white! So please avoid asking him for an opinion. His last date was white, they went to a formal restaurant wearing black and grey and ate white chicken with grey wilting veggies…'

SNAP! Zain shut his laptop with a bang. 'Enough! Get off your ass and get out of here. We should have left you back home!

'Ashar, let's get ready. *Daadijaan* has asked us to escort her to the *nikaah* ceremony. So let's get our act together. Do you need any help with your *shervani?*' Zain pointed at the long traditional jacket that Ashar was wearing, 'after all, I am your best man.'

'*Nahin, yaar*! All under control. You go and get ready—into your grey or black *shervani*. *Daadijaan* chose it especially for you. I had told her to get you a maroon one like mine, but she said, "Zain—*woh toh black ya grey hi pahenega!*" Come to think of it, Saif was right! Ha ha...' He cut off his laugh as he caught Zain glaring at him.

Alone in his room, Zain quickly changed into his clothes for the *nikaah* and reopened his laptop. He was in the middle of a deal and needed to get some work done. There was too much on his mind. This deal in London would be very important for the company and would help them expand in the UK as well, his phone beeped just then, a quick glance towards the screen showed Rachel's name. They had just broken up; he had always maintained it was a casual relationship, while she had started wanting more. Zain wasn't interested, so he just ignored it—there was no way he was ready to get tied down now. Tapping away at his keyboard, sending off one email after another, Zain's face was a study in concentration.

They had been here in Dehradun for the past two days and everyday some ceremony or ritual was taking place, once for Saniya and once for Ashar. It had been quite hectic. He had a backlog of work he needed to get done. There had hardly been any time to even turn on his computer, Indian weddings were known for their excessive festivities—all revolving around music, dance, and food, and yes, ceremonies. Unlike his brother, Zain shook his head and thought all of it to be a tad bit excessive. Why couldn't it just be a one-day affair, a simple ceremony and a reception like they had back home in the US?

Just then, Ashar popped his head around the door, 'Zain! Not again—come on let's go!'

Zain and Ashar walked towards Daadijaan's room. *Daadijaan* was waiting for them, all dressed in a traditional *sharaara* in off-white lace and gold. Her hair covered with a veil, she had delicate earrings dangling from her ears and gold and pearl bangles on her narrow wrists. *Daadijaan* looked thrilled to see her two eldest grandsons arriving to escort her to the ceremony. She looked at them proudly, beaming at them—they made her so proud!

Linking her arm into theirs, each flanking her on either side, they walked slowly to the venue.

[4]

All heads turned as the two handsome men walked their *Daadijaan* up to the stage set-up for the ceremony. The *nikaah* was to start in a few hours, and now the family was just sitting around, meeting friends, and relatives who had all come in for the wedding. They had deliberately kept the *nikaah* ceremony intimate, for just the immediate family. Guests were arriving later in the evening for the dinner, and a big reception was planned in Delhi as well. So, at that point, only family from both sides was present.

Daadijaan walked slowly towards the stage. Her sons, Walid and Armaan, and Saniya's father, Anwar, were waiting at the steps to greet her. *Daadijaan* was quite a personality: regal, revered, and respected by all. As she neared the steps to the stage, she suddenly stopped. Both Ashar and Zain looked down at her as they realised that she had stopped. Anwar, Armaan, and Walid also looked towards her...

'*Daadijaan*, are you alright?' whispered Zain.

'*Kya Huan, Daadijaan?*' asked Ashar softly.

But *Daadijaan* didn't move. Her grip on their arms hardened. No one dared move.

The three older men on the other side had questioning looks on their faces. Looking from *Daadijaan* to the strapping men flanking her. But *Daadijaan* didn't move.

'I will not go on the stage,' she announced, ' nor will my boys.' There was stunned silence all around. Even the *Maulvi*, who had arrived to conduct the ceremony, was looking confused.

'*Daadijaan*, what are you saying?' muttered Ashar.

Zain looked down at his grandmother with a puzzled look on his face.

'Yes, neither I, nor my grandsons will step on that stage until my demand is met!' she said.

Everyone's eyes widened in shock. What was the old lady saying?

Walid and Shaziya, Saniya's parents, started to look very worried. Were there some demands that they had to meet? There had been no discussion about this—what was this happening now just before the ceremony?

Anwar and Armaan were also left standing there, mouths agape.

Zain muttered, '*Daadijaan*, what is this rubbish you're talking about? What demand?'

'I will not permit Ashar to marry Saniya until my grandson, Zain, is also married.'

'WHAT! *Daadijaan*, have you lost it?' Zain's deep voice cut through the silence.

'I know what I am saying, and no, I have not lost it! I am very serious and as the senior-most person in the family and the head of the family, the wedding cannot take place without my permission,' said *Daadijaan* placidly.

'But *Daadijaan*, all this is happening because you're the one who wanted it,' stuttered Ashar.

Anwar, Armaan, and their wives rushed towards their mother, trying to see if she was all right—a total cacophony all around.

But the old lady sat there like a statue, refusing to budge.

Finally, Zain spoke and told Ashar, 'Just get on the stage yourself and get married. Leave *Daadijaan* out of this—enough of this drama! *Daadijaan*, you cannot do this! I will not get married and cannot get married just now. So that is that! *Maulviji*, please start the ceremony!'

Ashar then spoke up, 'No, Zain, I cannot get married without *Daadijaan*'s permission.'

'What? What rubbish! *Daadijaan*, you cannot do this! You cannot blackmail us like this. *Baba, Chacha jaan,* how are you quiet?'

'If *Ammajaan* doesn't give permission, then we cannot go ahead with Ashar's wedding, Zain,' Armaan said slowly.

'Which world do you all live in? *Daadijaan*, do you realise what you are doing? Think about Ashar and the family, also think about Walid Uncle and Saniya. How can you do this to them?' Zaid railed.

Walid and his wife had tears in their eyes; they couldn't believe this was happening. Walid came up to *Daadijaan* with his hands folded, 'Please change your mind—it is a question of our daughter.'

But *Daadijaan* sat like a statue.

This went on for another half an hour, but *Daadijaan* did not budge. Zain was about to burst a blood vessel, pacing up and down in the corridor; Ashar and his father Armaan pacing around him, while Anwar was still trying to make his mother see reason. All the women were weeping or glancing around nervously. Jahanaara sat with a frown on her face. Her mother-in-law was up to something. She knew it! She always knew it when her mother-in-law wanted her way and wouldn't budge until she got what she wanted.

But this time, it was her son caught in the middle of this unreasonable storm. She wouldn't let this happen, though deep down, she knew that if her husband agreed, she wouldn't have any say at all. Her only hope was Zain—she just hoped he wouldn't give in.

Armaan finally went quietly up to his son. 'Zain, listen to me, you know *Ammajaan*—once she's decided on something, nothing will change her mind. Our only way out here is that you agree. Just agree, and then we'll see what to do later. Anyway, how can we get you married right now—where is the girl? Just agree, and let Ashar's *nikaah* happen. We'll deal with your *nikaah* later. Most likely *Daadijaan* will forget about it. Please just agree. We cannot do this to Walid and his family.'

Zain stood looking out at the wedding party on the lawn. His gaze went to Walid uncle and his wife, who were sitting there, looking completely shattered and confused. Even Saniya and all the girls had come out from inside the bungalow to gather around their parents, and there was a worried look on everyone's face.

Ashar went over to speak to Saniya and console her. What had *Daadijaan* done? How could she do this? Zain's gaze moved to his beloved grandmother. He loved her, but couldn't imagine that she had done this. His gaze moved back to Saniya and Walid uncle. He could hear his father telling him to agree, and that they would figure things out once Ashar's wedding was over. He started thinking, maybe he should agree for the time being, just so that things could move on. Anyway, where would they find a bride for him now, all of a sudden?

Swallowing quietly, he turned towards his father and fixed his steely gaze on him, 'Okay, *Baba*, I agree, I agree to *Daadijaan*'s terms. I agree to get married.'

Armaan looked at his son. He couldn't believe Zain had agreed. He looked towards his mother. What was she up to? He hoped his son wouldn't get completely trapped in the middle of his mother's games. He looked his son in the eye and nodded quietly.

Both father and son walked towards the stage. Armaan said, '*Ammajaan, theek hain, alright,* Zain has agreed. He will get married—but first, let us get Ashar's *nikaah* over with. Then we shall look for a girl, and when we find a girl Zain likes, we shall get them married as well.' He crouched next to his mother, taking her delicate hands in his. 'Please let this wedding go on.'

Daadijaan, took her hands away from Armaan, looked up at her eldest grandson. 'Zain! I am happy you have agreed. I knew you wouldn't let me down! *Maulvi ji,* there will be two *nikaah*s today—please prepare!'

Zain looked down sharply at his grandmother, 'Two? *Daadijaan,* I have agreed—isn't that enough for you? I will get married—but first, Ashar will complete his *nikaah*. Then I will find someone to marry, and we shall have that *nikaah* as well.'

Daadijaan looked straight ahead, 'No! Both will take place today. Yours first.'

There was a stunned silence all around again.

'*Daadijaan*, enough is enough!' burst Zain. 'How can I get married now? To whom shall I get married? Please don't be ridiculous!'

'I have a bride ready for you.'

'What?!'

'What?' came the response from everyone.

'*Kaun*? Who?'

'Sara.'

'Sara? Who is Sara?'

'Sara? My daughter Sara?' stammered Walid.

'Yes, your daughter Sara. I want Zain to marry her, and I will not take no for an answer.'

'B- but… Sara? She is a child—how can we do this?'

'Is she a child?' asked the *Maulvi*, who had been a quiet bystander throughout the episode. 'I am sorry, *Ammaji*. If she is a child, then the Indian Constitution doesn't permit underage marriages, and I cannot solemnise it.'

Daadijaan raised her hand to quieten the *Maulvi*, 'Do you think I would ask anyone to do anything illegal? Am I a fool?'

The poor *Maulvi* almost wilted under her gaze.

Zain muttered under his breath, 'Not a fool—but surely the devil!'

'Call Sara!' *Daadijaan* commanded.

Everyone looked around. Where was Sara?

'Who is this Sara?' Zain muttered.

Ashar replied, 'Saniya's youngest sister. She's a kid, yaar!'

Walid kept saying, 'But how can we get Sara married? She's still a child—*Ammaji*, she's my youngest... still in school... still a child.'

A bewildered Sara was located in her room and dragged out by her sisters. Though dressed in her *lehenga* for her sister's wedding, she was holding on to her history textbook.

This child! Was *Daadijaan* mad?! Zain looked at Sara—a medium height girl, with a mop of wavy hair, thin and really young. She couldn't be more than 15 or 16. Had she completely lost it? Thank God the *Maulvi* had refused, thought Zain.

'Sara is of age!' announced *Daadijaan*.

'What?' exclaimed Zain.

'Yes. Sara, how old are you?'

Sara, still looking confused and a little scared, stood in front of *Daadijaan* and her parents. 'I'm 18.'

What?!

Walid stammered, 'No, no, Sara isn't 18 yet, she'll turn 18 on the 15th of... Ma... rrr... cch.... today...' his voice diminished into a whisper.

With all the madness of the wedding preparations, everyone had forgotten that it was also Sara's 18th birthday. She was 18.

Sara was still looking around, bewildered. What was happening? She had realised there had been some hold-up for the wedding ceremony, so had quietly slipped away to sit with her books for a bit while everything was sorted. She had no idea why she had been frantically summoned, or why she was being asked all these vague questions....

Yes, they had forgotten it was her birthday, but after having lived away in boarding school for the past few years and with a bunch of older sisters, she was used to being ignored and forgotten. Anyway, she was very worried about her forthcoming exams. What had happened? Why was everyone looking at her?

Daadijaan looked around her smugly, 'There—I have a proper bride for you, Zain, and you shall marry her. M*aulviji*, Sara is 18. Will you now marry her and Zain?'

The *Maulvi*, suddenly realising he had an important role to play, smiled, joined his hands, and said he was the *apprentice of Allah*—and he could, as long as both boy and girl were agreeable.

He went and took his position on the stage.

Walid suddenly said, 'But I cannot let this happen. I cannot let my daughter get married like this.'

'Walid, then your elder daughter Saniya shall also not get married.'

Walid looked deeply worried.

Zain's deep voice spoke up again. '*Daadijaan*, do you realise that you're blackmailing us, you are forcing me to get married and forcing Walid uncle to agree to this. How can you do this?'

'Zain, I can and I will. Because, I know what's good for you—and for her. Trust me!'

'*Daadijaan*, she's a child...'

'And you're no doddering old man! There was a larger age difference between me and your grandfather, and we were very happy,' *Daadijaan* cut him off.

Walid suddenly spoke up, 'Okay, I agree. But though we shall have the *nikaah* now, I won't let Sara's *rukhsati* until she has completed her college studies—for the next five years. If you agree, *Ammaji*, then we can go ahead. Otherwise, we call the whole thing off. I don't want my Saniya to also get stuck in this!'

Saniya had tears streaming down her cheeks. Sara, who was beginning to understand what was happening, suddenly started shaking her head. 'No, *Abba*, what are you saying?' She looked at her eldest sister's face.

Walid turned to Sara, took her arm, and led her into a nearby room. There was a tense silence all around and a very tense atmosphere.

Walid made Sara sit down and told her to trust him. 'I won't send you off with them. Get married now, so Saniya can also get married. You'll stay with us, complete your education, and after five years we will see what to do. We can get the whole thing annulled—I am sure Armaan bhai will agree. But, as of now, I need you to agree… please!'

Sara couldn't believe what she was hearing. She didn't fully understand most of it either. She finally just lowered her eyes in consent.

She walked back with her father to the stage.

Walid looked towards *Daadijaan* and repeated what he'd said earlier, 'I agree to give my daughter Sara, but the *rukhsati* will happen after five years, after she has completed her studies. We shall not speak of this *nikaaah* until that time. *Ammaji*, do you agree with this?'

Daadijaan slowly looked from Walid to Armaan, and then from a seething Zain to a quiet, head-bowed Sara. She turned towards the *maulvi* and announced, 'First read the *nikaah* for Zain and Sara, and only then Ashar and Saniya. Yes, I am agreeable.'

[5]

Early in the morning on 16th of March, the day after all the drama in Dehradun, Zain drove out of the city towards Delhi. The rest of the family were going to spend the next week in Delhi for Ashar and Saniya's Valima, or reception, and would then fly back to the States. As soon as he approached the outskirts of Delhi, the driver turned the car towards the international airport. He was taking the next flight out to London, then Paris, and finally New York. He had made a few calls to his London office; they weren't expecting him till the end of next week, but he had changed his plans. He couldn't stay on for another minute. It was stifling. He couldn't imagine what his beloved *Daadijaan* had made him do. He couldn't believe how the events had unfolded that evening. He had found himself sitting next to the *maulvi* agreeing to marry a girl he didn't know at all.

His father had said they would discuss this and find a solution once they were back in the US and after they had thought things through with a clear mind. From his point of view, the matter was closed. He wasn't going to think about it for another minute and he would act as though it had never happened. He wanted to wipe it out of his memory and life – and legally it would be as well – once the family was back in the States.

He had immersed himself in work and spent his evenings enjoying life with friends in London and Paris before flying home. Once back in New York, he had become very busy with the expansion of the business in Europe and was constantly flying back and forth. A few months after the family's return, he got a call from his father, asking him to come home to San Francisco for *Eid*. Zain wasn't religious, though he made it a point to visit the mosque once during Ramadan and pray with his family on *Eid*. So he headed home for the weekend. *Daadijaan* had come to the US with the family from India and he also wanted to discuss the situation with his father and find a solution to this problem.

It was good to be home after seven months; he was exhausted with all the travel and work and was yearning for some good home cooked food that he knew would also be there since it was *Eid*. He also wanted to spend time with his brother and sisters; he hadn't seen them since the trip to India, Saif having joined his MBA School at Stanford, and the twins were at UCLA—so it was a full house after a long time.

He used his key to open the door to the large, stately house his parents had built many years ago and often said was now too big for them, with none of the kids home and just them and the dogs—one being Zorro, his own . He loved being home, but after four or five days needed to get away to his own personal refuge, his own pad, just him. *Ammi* often said he had stayed away too long now and had gotten used to just himself. He loved the aroma of a *biryani* being cooked, or the elaichi chai that *Daadijaan* would brew, though even these had reduced as his parents had also gotten used to living in the US and a quick pasta or a lasagne was eaten more often than traditional Indian food, unless Daadijaan was visiting India. Today he could smell *biryani* and the *sheer khurma*; after all, it was going to be *Eid*! He walked through the house to find *Baba* and *Ammi* saying their prayers and *Daadijaan* meditating in her room as well. He could hear the basketball being thumped in the backyard, so he went out to join his brother and sisters. They were overjoyed to see him, though he could feel a little bit of tension in the air.

As the family sat around the *iftar* table after their *Eid* prayers, chatting and joking and sharing each other's news, a lull settled over the conversation. The tension was apparent, and then there was silence. *Daadijaan* broke the silence, 'I spoke to Ashar today, Saniya and he went to Maldives for their honeymoon and have been very busy organising their new home after their return. They were very happy.' She asked, 'Zain, have you spoken to Ashar?'

'No *Daadijaan*, I haven't spoken to anyone since I returned.'

She replied, 'Yes, not even to me.'

'*Daadijaan*, did you think I would after what happened?'

She replied, 'Why, what has happened?'

Shocked, Zain looked around at his family, who were all looking down at their laps, only his father and mother after a while looked at *Daadijaan*.

'*Daadijaan*, you tricked me into getting married to someone I don't even know!'

'So what? Even though I didn't know your grandfather, even your parents didn't know each other, everything is fine!'

'But, *Daadijaan*, those days were from a different era, things are different now, you don't play with people's lives like this!'

'Everything is a game. You have to take risks and sometimes they work and sometimes they don't. The ones that don't, don't because not much effort is made to make them work.'

'*Daadijaan*, I love you a lot, but I will not forgive you for this! Speaking of this... *Baba*, we need to meet the lawyer and see how we can get this annulled. Do you think Mr. Bakshi will be able to help us? We might need a *Shariyat* lawyer to help get this sorted out.'

Before Armaan could respond to his son, *Daadijaan* burst out, 'NO! This is not the way, the *nikaah* will not be annulled, at least not in my lifetime!'

Zain glared at his *Daadijaan*, 'I am sorry, I will not go through with this. I want out.'

'If you do this, Zain, you will see my dead face!'

'Oh please! *Daadijaan*, this isn't a Bollywood film—this is my life!'

'I repeat—you will see my dead face,' *Daadijaan*, stood up, pushed back her chair and went into her room and sat down on her prayer mat and started to tell her beads.

Zain looked at his parents, his father shook his head, and his mother pursed her lips and looked the other way, Saif and the girls quietly moved away.

Zain glared at them, shook his head, and stormed off into his room.

The next day, Zain joined his father at their San Francisco office and worked the entire day.

When they returned home at the end of the day, they found his mother frantic, *Daadijaan* had not spoken to anyone and nor had she eaten anything since the previous day and this was after a month of fasting.

She wouldn't budge. Finally Zain and Armaan asked her what she wanted, and in her crisp voice, she said, 'No annulment—not for the next five years at least.'

Reluctantly they agreed. Armaan spoke to Sara's father the next day and extended his support for the next five years and informed them that there would be no annulment.

The atmosphere in the house remained strained for the next few days, and eventually, everyone went their own ways.

[6]

Sara looked out of the window next to her. She could see the landing strip ahead. In another two hours, she would be where she had always dreamed of going. Boston University. She had worked very hard, slogged her butt off through college to maintain high grades and finally had got through a programme in Contemporary Art History for a year at BU, after which there was a possibility of a project with a museum as well.

She had spent the past week in Delhi with her parents, who had come to spend time with her elder sister Saniya and her husband, Ashar. Saniya had just had a baby, and *Amma* had come to be with her. Her sister Seher was away working in Singapore and engaged to a Chinese guy who worked with her, and Sophia, her other sister, had become a designer and was setting up her own boutique in Delhi as well. Sara had done her bachelor's in History from the prestigious St. Stephen's College in Delhi and had lived in the college residence for the past three years, and had followed this up with a year's course at the National Museum in New Delhi, often going over to her sister's place whenever she had a break. She was very fond of them.

But now she was on her own, moving towards her dream. The past four years had passed very quickly. She had been buried under her books. Her course was tough, and she had to put in long hours to maintain her grades, spending most of her free time working and studying at the National Museum of Art as an intern throughout those three years. She actually hadn't had time to breathe. Her course after that had also been quite intense. Occasionally, her mind would wander to the events of 15th March, four years ago—especially on that day every year, as it was her birthday.

She would get two phone calls regularly if she wasn't home, one from her *Abba*, telling her he loved her and that he was proud of her, and one from *Daadijaan*—to wish her and she would video call and speak. Daadijaan would call on the 15th of every month, without fail, and ask if she was okay. Though Sara had been angry with *Daadijaan* for quite some time, she could never ignore her and didn't dare miss her calls; there was something endearing about the old lady. She never asked about *Daadijaan's* family in the US, and *Daadijaan* never told her either. The US branch of the family hadn't visited India since Saniya and Ashar's wedding. *Daadijaan* would spend half the year in the US and half the year in India and would ask her to go and meet her whenever she was here, which was easy, as Sara could see her when visiting Saniya and Ashar.

Every 15th March, Sara would call Saniya to wish her for her anniversary, and Saniya would look at her, and wish her for her birthday, hug her tight… and thank her. Both Saniya and Sara knew why.

But now, she was far away from everyone. She had a number in her notebook—Armaan uncle's—given by her father in case of an emergency, and she hoped never to use it.

Once she landed, Sara collected her luggage and headed outside. The College Admissions Officer had said someone would be there to meet her and two other students arriving at the same time. She found them easily, and they were soon speeding towards the university campus.

Sara looked at the beautiful American scenery outside the car window. This was her first time in the US; she had travelled before, but hadn't been here. She was loving it already. The fresh air, the yellow and orange leaves on the trees, and the clear blue skies. It reminded her of the skies of Dehradun—Delhi never got such blue skies.

Soon she was settled into her dorm room. She was a graduate student with a TRA and on a scholarship, so was given a room to herself, which overlooked the small garden in between the campus buildings. If she stretched out of her window, she could see the cobbled path that led all the way to her department building.

She did up her room with all her belongings and personal touches. She had brought two brightly coloured patchwork Indian-print bedspreads from her favourite store back home—*FabIndia*. She had some bright-coloured cushions in red and orange, and a lovely magenta rug spread right next to her bed. She put up fairy lights around her wall, a few picture frames of her family, and her prayer mat stood rolled to one side in a basket along with some dried flowers. She would pick some fresh flowers from those that had fallen off trees and always kept a mug filled with water and blossoms at the corner of her desk and their fragrance filled her little room. She had a shelf to one side on with her electric kettle and a little hot plate, where she sometimes made herself some *Maggi* or instant noodles. There were also little boxes with her stash of fragrant tea leaves—Darjeeling, *masala*, *kahwa*, and *elaichi chai*—chai was her weakness; she could drink it any time, and often had friends from her dorm drop in for some. They said the aroma lured them into her room and the bright vibe inside lifted their moods.

She was quiet, yet friendly, easy to talk to, and very welcoming, so soon she made a few friends. They hung out together when she wasn't in class or wandering through the local museums. She had changed a lot over the past few years. From the bubbly and chirpy girl she had been in school, she was now much more reserved, and quiet—though still friendly in nature.

Sara was waiting for a chance to make a trip to New York to see the MET. She had been planning this for some time and was hoping her project with the museum would be based there.

Not overtly religious, she had become almost agnostic, but still offered a quick thanksgiving prayer every Friday facing *Mecca*. After her prayers, she usually video called her parents and chatted with her sisters and their families. The chats were often chaotic and sometimes hilarious. Very often she just sat and listened to them—they always had so much to share.

She did too, but they rarely had the time or inclination to listen to her rhapsodizing about a lecture, or a gallery she had visited, or the *chai* she had made. Her *Abba* would usually ask if she was okay for funds and whether he should transfer some to her. This conversation would end with her saying she had enough—and she really did, her TRA was quite generous and on the 15th of every month, she saw a decent amount of money being transferred into her account, which she had initially assumed was from her father, but then found out it wasn't him, but Armaan uncle and *Daadijaan*. When she mentioned it to *Daadijaan* during one of their calls,

Daadijaan raised her hand and told her to not even discuss it. It was her gift to Sara, and no one questioned a gift from a grandmother to her granddaughter. So that was that.

Ten days after Sara arrived in Boston, her phone buzzed, and she saw Armaan uncle's name pop up. Her *Abba* had saved that number on her phone. She picked it up and spoke softly, hesitantly.

Yes, she was fine.

No, she didn't have any trouble getting to the university.

Yes, her classes had started.

No, she wasn't lost, and no, she was not having any trouble.

Yes, she had his number and would call if needed.

Yes she would try and make a trip to the west coast and meet them during her break.

Yes she would try to meet him when he came to Boston for work.

Bye-bye.

And that was that.

[7]

'Sara, *beta*, how are you?'

'*Daadijaan*, I'm fine. I've been very busy with classes and assignments.'

'There's a long weekend coming up—why don't you come to San Francisco? Armaan and I would love to see you.'

'No *Daadijaan*, I've a lot of work and can't afford to miss any classes. I'll definitely come soon,' replied Sara, trying to control her emotions. After all that had happened, how could they expect her to want to see them. After that evening—apart from *Daadijaan*—none of them had even spoken to her, let alone met her. Yes, Armaan uncle had spoken to her after she'd arrived in the US, but that was just a courtesy.

'*Theek hain*, if you don't come, then I shall come to see you,' came *Daadijaan*'s reply.

'B...ut...!'

'No but! I'll come to Boston—then will you meet me at least?'

Sara didn't know what to say. She just mumbled something that sounded like agreement.

That evening, while working on an assignment, Sara heard a ping on her phone. *Daadijaan* had messaged. She was going to be in Boston on Saturday morning and would spend the day with her and would leave for New York by evening. Sara sighed and turned to look out of the window.

The more she tried to forget those memories and distance herself from everything associated with that evening—and how it had changed her life—the more she got stuck. She was married, but hadn't seen her husband for more than ten minutes and that too almost five years ago. There had been no attempt to meet or contact her—neither by him nor his family—apart from *Daadijaan*.

That evening had changed her life—from that of a schoolgirl worried about her studies and what she'd do with her future—the youngest in the family…. She should have had a carefree life, but no, she had spent the past years with her father looking at her with a look seeking forgiveness, becoming over protective, putting a strain in her relationship with everyone in her family; she couldn't believe they had agreed to make her go through with it.

Tomorrow she would be meeting *Daadijaan*, and the memories of that evening would again flood her mind…

Saturday came too quickly. Sara woke up, finished all her assignments, and changed into a nice bright *kurta* and a pair of jeans. Wrapping a stole around her neck, she picked up her bag and headed out of the dorm. She was meeting *Daadijaan* at a café near the museum. As she stepped out of the building, she suddenly heard her name being called. She looked up and saw the elegant, stately lady standing next to someone equally well-dressed, wearing a dark overcoat. He looked a little like Anwar uncle—Saniya's father-in-law. He must be Armaan uncle—her father-in-law.

She didn't remember him too well; hell, she didn't remember anyone at all! She had refused to see any photographs from that evening, or for that matter, any photographs connected to Saniya's wedding either. She had blocked Saniya's family from her Facebook and had not felt the need to ever search for any of those people on social media.

Sara smiled and walked slowly towards them. She hadn't expected *Daadijaan* to come with Armaan uncle. As she reached them, *Daadijaan* enveloped her into her arms. Sara was a little wary, a little tense—but in a few seconds, she melted in *Daadijaan*'s arms. She felt like she'd come home. A rush of emotion hit her—she suddenly missed her family. When finally *Daadijaan* let go of her, Sara straightened up and gently nodded at Armaan uncle, who smiled at her. He, too, was looking at her with a lot of emotion in his eyes.

'I was coming to meet you *Daadijaan*, you needn't have come till the campus,' said Sara, when they were finally all in the car and the driver was steering it towards the museum area.

'*Aarey*, how could we let you travel alone? We're early, so we decided to pick you up—and we're glad we did. It is nippy—you'd have caught a cold,' said *Daadijaan* affectionately.

They settled into the café and ordered coffee and food, *Daadijaan* did all the talking, while Armaan uncle kept quiet, occasionally asking her a question or two. Sara smiled, and answered all their questions and chatted with them. Thankfully, no one mentioned anything connected to that evening. *Daadijaan* kept talking about everyone in San Francisco how lovely their house was.

Daadijaan had now, on this trip, been in the US for five months and was hoping to return to India in a few months, before it became too cold in the US. She didn't like coming to the East Coast—it was too cold and windy—and she preferred the sunny locales of the west.

Soon, it was evening, and *Daadijaan* and Armaan uncle had a flight to catch to NYC. Sara bade them farewell and headed back to campus. It had been nice to meet them—but she was glad it was over. Exams were around the corner, and she had a lot to do.

'Armaan, what did you think of Sara?'

'What did I think, *Amma*? She's grown up.'

'Yes, she isn't that schoolgirl she used to be.'

'Yes, she's polite and soft-spoken, and despite everything, *Amma*, she wasn't rude or disrespectful at all. If I'd been in her place, I'd have refused to meet any of us.'

'See that, Armaan, is *tarbiyat* - Upbringing. For that, one must give full credit to Walid and Shaziya. Despite everything, they've taught her to be respectful. Sometimes, when I think back to how I behaved that evening, I feel like killing myself!'

'You do, *Ammajaan*? Thank God! Though I can't believe you're admitting it.'

'Why shouldn't I admit it? I overdid it—I admit it. But, I still think I made the right decision. What do you say?'

'*Amma*, please do not make any more schemes. Jahanaara still hasn't forgiven either of us for that evening. She doesn't say much to you, but I have to constantly hear her rant—and Zain has locked himself away, buried in his work.'

'All hogwash! Don't worry—it'll all work out. I think it's about time you speak to Walid and discuss bringing Sara home.'

'What?? *Ammajaan*, are you mad? I spoke to him about an annulment after five years. There's still a little time to go. Zain is now 30—he's waited long enough in this mess, just like Sara, I don't think we should meddle in their lives anymore! And by we, *Ammajaan*, I mean you.'

'At my age, it isn't called meddling—it's called setting things right!'

[8]

Sara had almost completed a year and a half at BU and had just been informed that she and two other batchmates had been selected for an internship and project—a sort of scholarship, and a continuation and culmination of her training and studies—at the MET in New York.

She had been overjoyed—this was what she'd worked so hard for!

That evening, she had a video call with her parents and shared the news. They were overjoyed, and her father told her he was very proud of her. She'd need to leave for New York at the end of the month. The university would pay her a stipend; she'd be able to learn from the best and also work on projects under them. The only thing she needed to do was to find a place to stay in NYC.

'But *beta*, how will you stay all by yourself in New York City? It's the biggest city in the world!' her mother exclaimed.

'*Ammi*, I'm staying by myself here in Boston too, *na*? Why are you panicking now?'

'That's different... you're living in the university dorm—it is safe and protected.'

'Oh God, *Ammi! Abba*, talk to her, please!'

'Okay, okay, Sara, let me figure this out. I'll speak to you in a few days. You concentrate on wrapping up.' Her father tried to make peace, but Sara knew her mother would chew his brain.

The week went by in a whizz. Sara had so much work to do, she barely noticed the days pass, and suddenly, only a few remained before she had to head to NYC. Her classmates, who'd also got the same project and internship, had asked if she wanted to join them in renting an apartment. She'd said she would speak to her family in India and let them know. But internally, she doubted they'd approve—both her classmates were men. Her mother would have a heart attack if she found out she was going to be sharing a flat with two men! Sara smiled, imagining her mother fainting if she heard. She was sure her father would figure something out—she was meeting them on Zoom that night.

'Hi *Abba*!' Sara smiled and waved at her parents as they appeared on her laptop screen.

'Sara, how have you been? All set?' asked her father.

'Yes, *Abba*, more or less…' Sara began replying.

Just then, she saw *Daadijaan* and Armaan uncle appear on the screen too.

Wooah!! She looked questioningly at her parents.

Everyone exchanged pleasantries.

Daadijaan smiled at Sara and said, 'Sara, when do you leave for New York? Your father told us the good news a few days ago.'

'Thank you, *Daadijaan*, I have to join work on Monday, so yes, four days to go.'

'Sara, about your living in New York—' her father started.

'*Abba*, my two classmates, Jon and Kevin, are also moving to New York. They have asked me to move into the flat they will take, we can share the rent, etc.' Sara chirped in.

'What?!' she heard her mother and *Daadijaan* both exclaim at the same time.

She'd expected her mum to react like this, but having *Daadijaan* and Arman uncle on the call complicated everything even further... Why were they even on this call?

'*Beta*,' her father cleared his throat, '*Beta*, you know we wouldn't be comfortable with you living with some strange, unknown men.'

'Well, *Abba*, I don't know anyone in New York—so I'll have to look for a place on my own,' Sara sighed.

'You will stay with Zain!' *Daadijaan* interrupted her as she spoke.

Sara stopped talking. 'What?'

'Yes, you cannot live by yourself in a city like New York—and definitely not with some unknown strange men!'

Sara looked at her parents. Her mother was nodding, and her father was looking at her but avoiding her gaze.

'Yes, Sara, you can stay with Zain. He lives in the heart of town, quite close to your workplace, and his apartment is large,' Armaan uncle also added.

Sara was in shock. What were they saying? She spoke up, 'Abba, you all have a problem with me living with strange people, but now you're suggesting that I live with Zain? I don't know him either—he's just as much a stranger to me as are Jon and Kevin, whom I've at least known for the past year and a half.'

'What are you saying, beta?' Daadijaan spoke in her clear, authoritative tone, 'Zain isn't a stranger—you've known him for the past five and a half years, and he is your husband!'

'Husband! Please—he isn't my husband, or anyone to me! That entire episode was a mistake, and something that shouldn't have happened. Please don't do this, *Abba*!'

'Sara, he is your husband, and if you're going to live and work in New York, then this is your only option. You'll stay with him. There—I've said it. The matter is closed!' Her mother piped in.

'But, but, *Abba, Daadijaan,* Armaan uncle—that isn't fair I have worked so hard to get this project! Please don't make me give it up!' Sara pleaded.

Daadijaan again spoke. 'Sara, your parents and we have already discussed this. This is the best option—the only option.'

'But, *Abba*,' Sara started.

'Sara, it's either this, or you'll have to give up the internship and come back,' her father cut in. 'That is the only solution we have,' he continued. She could detect a tinge of desperation in his tone. 'Let's know your decision by tomorrow morning. *Khuda Hafiz*!'

And with that, Sara was left looking at a blank screen—her father had ended the call.

Stunned by the sudden turn in events, Sara sat back. How did this happen? How could they even suggest that she would live in Zain's house? She shook her head. They weren't suggesting—they were dictating.

Sara went for a walk to clear her head. She desperately wanted this internship—it meant everything to her. It was a fabulous opportunity!

She didn't come from a particularly conservative family—after all, her own sister was working in Singapore. She was living with three colleagues who had been given accommodation by her company. And she was now engaged to a Chinese man and her family had not objected. She had known they would not take to the sharing of the apartment in NYC with unknown men—but had not for the life of her had she imagined that this would be their solution.

Sitting down on a bench near the dorm, Sara's mind also wandered to Zain—how had he agreed? He, who had left the very next morning after the *Nikaah* without looking back, never tried to get in touch or make an attempt to even speak to or meet her and her family. She refused to believe that he had willingly agreed. *Daadijaan* must have again forced him into this like she had forced the *Nikaah*.

Sighing, Sara, walked back to her dorm. She really didn't have a choice. She needed to stay here in the US, and at the moment, this was the only option she had.

[9]

'What?'

'Zain, think with a clear head… Sara's been doing her course at BU and now has to move to NYC to do her internship. She can't live with the two classmates—as they're men… as in she was okay with it, but her family and more so *Daadijaan*—*won't* permit it.'

'So?'

'So, Zain—*Daadijaan* wants her to stay with you. Her family agrees.'

'Why would I agree to let her stay with me?' Zain snapped back.

He suddenly heard *Daadijaan's* voice (Shit—*Baba* had put her on speaker), 'Because, she is in your *nikaah* and it is not right that she looks for another place to stay when you live in the same city. She is your wife—your responsibility!'

'What wife and what responsibility? One that was forced on me—by you, *Daadijaan*—she's your responsibility, not mine.'

Daadijaan's voice rose, 'Don't talk to me like that, Zain. It is a fact—she is in your *nikaah*, and your wife!'

Zain let out a string of expletives.

'Zain, Zain!' his father cut in. 'Look, Sara has worked very hard for this internship—it was a very tough competition. She needs to live in NYC and this is her only option.'

'I don't care!'

'Zain, if you do not agree, she will have to return to India and give up the internship and the opportunity she has been given. Don't be selfish. Think about it.'

His father continued, 'She was completely against this entire idea as well and was going to live with two of her male classmates who are also coming to NYC with her. But her parents—especially *Daadijaan*—wouldn't permit it.'

'Zain, she doesn't deserve to lose such an opportunity—you know that. Listen, she needs to start her internship on Monday. Today is Friday. Let me know in a few hours. You'll need to go and pick her up from Boston.'

Cursing loudly, Zain hung up..

He was standing on the deck in his apartment. He breathed in and out a few times to calm his nerves and then picked up the drink he'd been nursing when his father called.

Taking a few sips, Zain looked out into the open dark space in front.

Shit.

He couldn't believe this was happening. He had tried to wipe that entire episode from his life and had worked very hard to forget it. He hadn't tried to find out anything about the girl he had been forced to marry. He knew his grandmother was in touch and hell, his cousin Ashar was married to her sister, but he had never once asked about her and his family hadn't actually visited India after that. All the business trips to India had been made by his father or handled by his uncle and Ashar. Clenching and unclenching his fists, Zain ran a hand through his hair and shook his head.

Picking up his phone, he dialled his father.

'Send me her number and address, *Baba*!'

His phone buzzed as soon as he'd disconnected the call. *Baba* had sent Sara's contact number and address. She was at BU—four hours away. He could leave in the morning and then could get back by evening. She'd get a day to settle in before she started work and he would also be able to get back to his normal life.

The next morning, Zain changed into a pair of jeans and a shirt, picked up his car keys and left home, a hundred thoughts racing through his mind. Sudden flashes of the nightmare that was the evening in Dehradun. The evening his entire life had turned into a full-fledged Bollywood drama. His forced *nikaah* to Sara, a girl much younger than him, someone he didn't even know, had never seen before and hadn't seen or heard of since then. So she was the one *Baba* and *Daadijaan* had gone to meet in Boston some months ago. When they had surprised him with a visit on Saturday night, he had been out with friends and was stumped to find them waiting for him at his apartment when he had returned. He thanked his lucky stars that he had returned alone, otherwise he would have had a night full of questions by *Daadijaan*.

Sara... where had she emerged from? She had been a kid back then and couldn't be much older now...

Oh God, he would have to babysit her now—that was all he needed!

Zain shook his head, trying to push the jumbled thoughts from his mind as he sped across the freeway towards Boston. It was going to be a long day!

As he drove into the campus, he checked his watch—it was 9 am. He'd made good time. A cup of coffee was what he needed desperately. As he drove towards the location on his phone, he glanced around the streets. College campuses always reminded him of his days at UCLA and Stanford. Those were good days.

Zain tried to decide whether he should stop for his coffee before reaching the dorm or whether he should head there straight, after all, they would need to eat before they headed back.

As he parked in front of the dorm, he called the number his *Baba* had sent him.

Sara answered on the third ring. 'Hello?'

There was a pause on the other side for a couple of seconds. And then a very deep voice spoke, 'I'm downstairs at the reception. Could you come down with your luggage please?'

Zain waited for a response. After what felt like an eternity, 'Alright, give me five minutes please,' whispered the voice at the other end.

Stretching his legs and his back, Zain waited outside, leaning against the hood of his car, looking around, trying to locate a café open somewhere nearby. He needed that coffee.

The swish of the dorm doors opening pulled his attention back to the entrance. A figure in a bright red jacket and jeans with a green woollen cap covering the entire head came out walking backwards, dragging two big suitcases behind her. She stopped at the entrance, looked around, and spotted him. Not that it was hard—he was the only one there. He stood up and moved towards her, reaching out to help her with her suitcases.

'Sara?'

The green-capped, dark-glasses-donned face nodded.

Once they had the bags settled at the back of his SUV, Sara, stood by the car, looking a little nervous. She couldn't see him very clearly—his shades covered his eyes and all she could see was a grim face below that. He didn't even look familiar— not that she remembered what he looked like. Zain slid into the driver's seat and unlocked the other side for her, motioning her to get in. Sara climbed in, and automatically reached for the seatbelt....

Suddenly, cutting through the silence, he said, 'Is there a café close by?'

Sara almost jumped out of her skin. Trying to recover, she said, 'Y-es, just down the road and to the right.'

Zain gripped the steering wheel and put the car into motion, her voice was a little muffled, but he could hear what she had said. He really needed that coffee.

They got out and headed indoors, the elderly man behind the counter smiled and waved at Sara. Ambling over, he asked, 'Why are you still here, Sara? I thought you had to join your internship in NYC on Monday.'

Sam smiled at her again and then asked, 'Is this your man here, Sara?'

'My man? Oh... uhh... mmm...'

'One strong coffee—and whatever you've for breakfast that is healthy, please!' cut in that same deep baritone.

Uncle Sam turned his head towards Zain, eyes darting towards Sara, 'Oh sure, we've muesli and some home-baked sourdough with fresh fruit. Sara, what will you have?'

'A cup of tea and a bagel please, Uncle Sam!'

Flashing them a smile, Uncle Sam bustled off.

Silence.

Zain began scrolling through his phone. Sara looked away outside the window at the street where people were still waking up, going for a run, starting their day late as it was the weekend.

They ate in silence, Zain paid the bill, and then left after Sara bade Uncle Sam goodbye one last time, wishing them safe health.

Just as they were leaving Boston, Zain's phone buzzed.

'*Baba.*'

'Zain, have you managed to pick up Sara and leave Boston?'

'Yes, we are on our way.'

'Be careful. Drive safe. I'll let Walid know in India.'

'*Ji*, okay.'

'Call once you reach – *Allah haafiz!*'

'*Ji.*'

Zain disconnected the call and once again focussed on the road. This time Sara's phone buzzed. She looked at her screen—*Daadijaan*. Glancing at Zain, she took the call.

'*Salaam aleikum, Daadijaan!*'

'*Walaikum assalam, beta,* are you alright?'

'Yes, *Daadijaan.*'

'There is nothing to be afraid of, don't worry—you are now with Zain. All will be well. He is my responsible grandson.'

'*Ji.*'

'I'm very relieved as well. Armaan will inform your father in India, *theek hain, okay!* Stay safe and call once you reach home. *Allah hafiz!*'

Sara turned her head away to look outside. Home. Zain's home was the last place she wanted to be. Tears filled her eyes. She quickly pushed her dark glasses back up her nose, turning to glance at Zain only once she had them on. Apart from a grim expression on his face, she couldn't make anything out. He had his own shades.

Sara thought, it must not be easy on him either—she was sure he didn't want to do this at all. After all, he hadn't even laid eyes on her, let alone contact her, in the past three and a half years. She didn't blame him, the entire mess that happened that evening had been extremely harsh on both of them... and totally unfair.

After another hour of silence, Sara started feeling a little drowsy shifted about, trying to find a comfortable angle to rest her head. The road ahead was straight and seemed endless, creating a lull.

'Push it back and adjust,' the deep baritone made her jump. She looked at him startled.

'Push back the seat and adjust the backrest.' Zain repeated, grimacing as he spoke. 'The lever is to your right.'

'Thank you,' Sara did as she was told and found a comfortable angle. Slowly closing her eyes, she drifted off to sleep.

After ten minutes, Zain turned on some music, keeping the volume low, so as to not disturb Sara as she slept. He glanced at her to check she was still asleep. Her cap had slipped off. This was perhaps the first time he had actually properly looked at her. Her eyes were still covered by her glares, but he could see her jet-black hair near her forehead. She seemed to have tied it up into a ponytail as most of it was still in the cap that hung low on her head. She had clear skin, a shade of frothy coffee, with a tint of red on her cheeks with the cold and a button-like nose. Nothing unusual. Nothing dramatic. His eyes moved lower and then stopped. Her lips had parted. She had no lipstick or gloss on. He hadn't seen many women without any make up—other than his mother and sisters— and they didn't count. He had seen many women early in the morning, but that didn't matter as well; they had been busy with other distractions. Zain's grimace changed slightly into a little smile at the thoughts going through his head. He felt himself drawn to her sleeping form. His eyes went back towards her face. Her lips—there was something about them… Sara had her face at an angle towards the window, and the sun's rays were falling on her face, making her nose glow, highlighting her lips. Which she unconsciously licked with her tongue in her sleep. He felt a kind of magnetic attraction to that sight.

Zain banged his fists on the steering wheel, accidentally hitting the horn. Sara jumped in her sleep, suddenly being woken out of deep slumber. She hadn't slept all night in anxiety after Armaan uncle had called—and the straight, never-ending road hadn't helped.

As she got her senses back and glanced around, it took her a few seconds to get her bearings, quickly glancing at the ramrod straight grimacing man next to her. Her eyes moved to notice his clenched fists on the steering wheel. His knuckles were white. It looked like he was gripping the wheel in anger.

Sara sat up and readjusted her seat. 'Thank you...,' she finally spoke softly, after ten minutes.

'Are you talking to me?' replied the deep baritone.

Sara turned towards him, 'Yes. Thank you for coming to get me. I wish you hadn't been forced to.'

'I have been forced to do many things in my life... let us add this to the list.'

Zain's face didn't let anything on; just grim and firm; hands still rock hard on the steering wheel.

Sara quietly turned away and sat looking out of the window. Her eyes filled with tears. She was thankful for her glares. She pulled up the collar of her jacket to try and cover her face and quivering lips and adjusted her woollen cap to cover her head.

The rest of the trip passed in silence. It was a long drive to NYC.

[10]

It was almost sunset by the time they entered New York; they had driven without a break, except for a stop to refuel, freshen up, and grab a coffee.

Zain pulled into a drive-in and picked up two Subway sandwiches, which they ate as he manoeuvred the car through the city.

Sara tried to spot sights with the setting sun in the background. She couldn't believe she was in New York City—not like this. Her thoughts turned to the list of places she had noted down in her diary, when she was planning her visit, and sighed.

Zain glanced towards her, hearing the sigh. 'We should be there in five minutes. Do you need anything else to eat?' he spoke in a low voice.

Sara shook her head. She wanted nothing—and definitely not this.

Zain parked in his usual spot in the basement. They had pulled into the basement parking of a fancy apartment complex. It looked like a tall building... but that was all she could make out. She had no idea where they were exactly.

Zain helped her push her suitcases into the elevator and he stood in front of her near the door. She couldn't see which button he pressed as they entered. A little nervous, she quickly glanced up to see the numbers light up as they passed floors. The lift moved quickly, and her ears popped. This must be one of those super-fast elevators. They finally stopped and the doors slid open on the 30th floor. Sara felt dizzy just at the thought of being so high up and instinctively reached out to hold on to the wall.

She followed Zain out of the lift, dragging the smaller suitcase, her gaze towards the floor. Bump! She had bumped into something. She looked up to find it was Zain, who had stopped in front of her to swipe his key to open the front door.

'Sorry,' she muttered, lowering her eyes as he turned around to look at her, his face still grim and frowning.

She walked into the apartment and dragged her suitcase to where Zain had left the one he'd been pulling. Taking a deep breath, she looked around. Zain had moved ahead. He opened a door and she could hear him tell her that she could use his study for her things and that there was a pull-out bed she could use. She moved towards the room he'd entered, trying to catch everything he was saying, still looking around to get her bearings, when BUMP! Again, she'd bumped into something—or someone... She felt herself slipping backwards, when two strong hands held on to her and helped her regain her balance.

'Sorry, thank you,' muttered Sara as she straightened herself.

Zain stepped back and let her walk past him into his study. He'd bought this studio apartment a few years ago. It was a large apartment for a studio and was on two levels. The lower level had an open kitchen, and a spacious, airy living room and dining space which opened out into a large deck overlooking Central Park. They were high enough to get an uninterrupted view of an expanse of green. This was something he loved for it reminded him of his parents' home in San Francisco. Every room in that house opened onto the garden. There was a small room at the back of the lower level which is where he had set up a study-office and had a couch which opened into a bed. That bed had been only used by Saif the few times he had visited. His parents usually stayed at the fancy hotel that was down the street.

Most of his other visitors had shared his bed. His bedroom was the entire upper floor with a huge walk-in closet and large bathroom. The room felt larger because he had bought himself a queen-sized bed. He liked his bed to be cosy. To one side were full length glass doors that opened out into another small deck that overlooked the deck at the lower level. He loved his apartment.

'Can I bring my suitcases into this room?' Sara's soft voice broke his thoughts.

'I will bring them in,' he pulled both suitcases inside the study effortlessly while she stood in the middle of the room looking around.

'There is a small powder room just outside. I am afraid the bath is upstairs, so you will have to use that.'

'Please don't worry, I will be fine.'

His eyes kept going to her lips. She seemed to be biting them.

'If you're sure you're not hungry, I am going to head upstairs. The fridge will have something in case you are hungry later.'

'Thank you.'

'Good night!'

Zain walked out of the room, went straight to his bar and poured himself a stiff whiskey, added some ice from the freezer and headed upstairs. He was exhausted and needed to unwind before he crashed.

Walking out on to his sit out, he took a sip from his glass and felt the golden liquid burn his throat. He winced as the whiskey slid down his throat. Taking a deep breath, he put his glass down and looked straight ahead. Something buzzed in his pocket. Reaching for his phone, he saw *Baba* flash on the screen.

'Zain, have you reached?'

'Yes, *Baba*, I was about to call you.'

'Good! Is Sara alright? Have you settled her in? Did you all eat something?'

'Yes, to all those questions, *Baba*. I am exhausted... I am going to crash. Will speak later, bye.'

'But, Zain...'

He could hear his father still talking when he disconnected.

He took another sip of his drink, rotating his neck trying to take some of the cricks out. His eyes moved down to the lower-deck, he could see the rest of his apartment from here. All the lights were dimmed. He could actually even see his study. The lights were on and someone was moving around—Sara.

She couldn't see him but he could see her. He saw her move towards the window. It had already become dark, so other than lights she couldn't see anything outside.

He saw her standing there with something shining in her hand. It must be her phone.

Sara was exhausted. She quickly used the washroom and made her bed. Zain had left some bedding on the couch which he had opened out for her. It wasn't very wide, but was quite firm as it was a leather couch and the cushions were turned over when it doubled into a bed.

She was about to crawl under the covers when she realised she needed to draw the curtains. Not that anyone would be able to look in. She got out of bed and walked towards the window. Her phone buzzed just then.

'*Daadijaan*' flashed across the screen. Sara rolled her eyes, shut them tight and sighed... sliding the talk button.

'*Salaam alaikum, Daadijaan*'

'Sara, have you reached and are you okay?'

'Yes, *Daadijaan*. All okay! We got here a little while ago and I was about to call you. Are you alright?'

'Yes, yes, what will happen to me? Armaan was speaking to Zain, so I thought I would speak to you. Just relax now, okay? Sleep well and tomorrow I will call you again. Don't worry, okay!'

'Yes, thank you. *Allah hafiz*!'

Sara looked out of the window. She could see lights on all three sides, but right in front was a dark mass, what was that? It couldn't be the sea, she couldn't smell it—what was it? She stood there for a while looking out, lost in thought. Finally, a firecracker bursting at a distance brought her back, and she quietly moved away from the window and crawled back into bed. She would think about everything tomorrow, now she needed to sleep.

[11]

Zain's eyes opened one at a time. Something was buzzing… and it wasn't stopping!

Groaning aloud, he reached towards his bedpost for the alarm, but it wasn't the alarm. He felt around the bed, trying to find the source of the buzzing. After a few seconds, he finally dug his phone out from under the covers. He had just managed to shower and crashed last night, which is why his hair was still slightly damp. He must have been really dog tired, he thought, looking at his phone, still a little groggy, he couldn't recognise the number that was flashing. It was an Indian number.

Who the hell? He quickly checked the time; it was 8 am

'Hello?'

'Zain?'

'Yes, this is Zain. Who is this?'

'Zain, *beta*, this is Walid, Sara's father. You may not recognise me, *beta*.'

'*Ji*, Uncle, good morning.'

'*Beta*, I wanted to thank you. You have really helped us. I don't know what I would have done and how Sara would have managed!'

'It's okay uncle, please don't worry.'

'Zain, *beta*, we are indebted to you—thank you.'

'*Allah hafiz*, Uncle.'

Zain was now fully awake. He sat in bed, looking down at his phone. For a few seconds after he had answered the phone and heard the voice on the other side, he was a little lost, and then suddenly, everything came rushing back to him.

Sara... he had driven to Boston and brought her to NYC, as dictated by his grandmother. She was to live in his apartment while she did her internship. He had just about managed to mutter a few responses on the phone to her father.

Taking a few deep breaths, Zain was about to close his eyes again when his phone buzzed—*Daadijaan*! Clamping his eyes shut, Zain sighed. Then, he got out of bed, moved towards the bathroom, and ignored his phone.

Five minutes later, he padded downstairs, walked straight to his kitchen and turned on his coffee maker. He needed a strong shot to begin his day and it had started quite early for a weekend, thanks to all the phone calls. He glanced towards his study, the door was shut, she must still be asleep. He had to head out to run some errands for a few hours, so he wrote down the address of the house and the landline number as well as the Wi-Fi password on a post and stuck it on the fridge, in case Sara needed it.

He was about to turn around and walk upstairs again, when he suddenly saw some movement from the corner of his eye. There was a white bundle curled up in the corner of his white couch. Sipping his coffee, he moved towards the couch wondering what it was, only to realise it was Sara, bundled up in the white blanket he had left for the previous night, curled up into the corner of the soft white couch in his living area. Why was she here and not in the study?

He stepped closer and could see a little bit of her face sticking out from under the covers. His eyes were drawn to her lips again. All he could see was that button of a nose and those lips. He guessed she needed to breathe, which is why that part of her was uncovered. Her lips parted as she slept and he couldn't keep his eyes averted. Should I wake her and ask her to go back to studying?

Shaking his head, he shut his eyes to get her lips out of his mind and moved away. Picking up his coffee he headed upstairs to change.

It was almost early evening by the time Zain got back home. He entered his home and expected to find Sara awake and there in the living room, but all was quiet. The white bundle was missing from the couch. He dropped his keys and hung his jacket up in the hall closet, and walked into the living room. There was no one there. Walking into the kitchen, he noticed two mugs had been washed and kept to dry, his morning coffee mug and another one. He walked around and stood quietly near the study door, but heard no sound from the other side. Maybe she was asleep...

Zain headed to the kitchen and poured himself a glass of water and headed upstairs to his room. He was browsing through his messages on his phone as he climbed the stairs when, BUMP! He crashed into Sara. His phone slipped and he instinctively reached out his arms to steady her. This is becoming a habit now!

Sara stood in front of him with a towel around her head—his towel—and another towel around her body—his towel...

'I am sorry! I went to take a shower and realised I didn't have a towel and had left my fresh clothes downstairs!' she blubbered, caught completely off guard. She hadn't expected him to be back at this time—frankly she had lost track of time.

Zain held up one of his hands to silence her blubbering, and realised his other hand was still holding on to her arm. He stood to one side to let her pass, 'Go and change, I will organise something for us to eat.'

Sara ran down the stairs, clutching on to the towels. Both towels were huge and kept her nicely covered, so she shouldn't have been worried. Sara quickly dried her hair and changed into a fresh orange sweatshirt and jeans. Running a comb through her damp hair and putting her regular dab of kajal to her eyes, Sara took a deep breath and opened the door of the study and walked out into the living area.

She saw Zain on his phone on the other side of the window. She realised he must be outside on a balcony or a sit out. Gingerly, she headed in the same direction, cautiously stepping out; she remembered they were on the 30th floor and just the thought of looking down from that height made her a little dizzy!

She was very quiet as she stepped onto the sit-out at the back and stood there, looking out. Zain was still on the phone. She could hear his deep voice as he spoke. Gingerly she took a few steps towards the other side, near the railing so that she could look out...

GASP! Sara looked out, straight in front of her, her mouth open…

Hearing her loud gasp, Zain turned around and his eyes went straight for her lips again. After a few seconds, he realised she had frozen, and was looking straight ahead.

'That's Central Park,' he said, covering his phone. He went back to speak into his phone and soon signed off.

He turned to Sara who was still rooted to the same spot.

'That is Central Park, you can see a lot of it from every room and window in the apartment,' he explained.

'So, this was the dark mass I could see from the window in the study. I was wondering what it was,' whispered Sara. Her eyes moved to her left and right; she couldn't believe that there could be such a green mass in the middle of this concrete jungle. She hadn't stepped out onto the deck the entire day, hadn't even looked out of the windows. She'd been so exhausted; she had slept most of the day.

Zain glanced at Sara. Many people had the same reaction as Sara. Hell, he had had the same reaction the first time he had come to see the apartment. And it had been one of the main reasons for him buying it.

'I have ordered some food for dinner. It should be here in a bit. Did you eat anything before this?'

'No, I just had some hot water. I woke up a little while ago, when *Daadijaan* called.'

Zain looked away. *Daadijaan* had called him a number of times as well, and he hadn't taken a single one of her calls. He was super pissed with her—if it wasn't for her he wouldn't have been in this situation!

Zain suddenly remembered, 'Your father had called this morning—I forgot to mention it!'

'*Abba* had called you?' Sara asked, turning her face towards Zain, her eyes a little teary and big.

This was the first time Zain had actually seen her face properly—without her shades, her jacket collar, a blanket or a towel covering it—oval in shape, with her damp hair framing it—her hair must be below her shoulder, a little button of a nose, her lips were still parted and his eyes moved to hers.

He shook himself. 'Yes, he called this morning to speak to me. I told him you were all right.'

'Yes, *Ammi* and *Abba* called me as well this morning, after I spoke to *Daadijaan*. Both had been calling many times, but I had left the phone in the study. It was only later that I saw all their missed calls before they called back. They wanted to see if I was okay.'

Sara kept talking.

Zain was quiet and listened, trying to not think of how her lips moved as she spoke.

Suddenly, his phone buzzed again. 'Mark! Hey, yes, I'm in town and home. How are you? When did you get in?'

Sara stopped talking as she heard Zain on the phone. She quietly moved back inside. It was a little chilly.

She moved to the kitchen area and opened the fridge. There was milk, eggs, some fruit, some preserves, and bread. She poked around a little further and found a few packets of prawns and some chicken in the freezer and lots of cheese of various kinds. She poked around the cupboards in the kitchen and found a whole shelf of various kinds of coffee and liquors, and even a wine closet—but not what she was looking for... She wondered what to do...

She turned around and saw Zain walking back inside, still on the phone, his deep voice clear but low, 'Let me pick Leyla up and we can meet you at your place in an hour. Chilling on your deck and having a drink sounds good. Great! See you then.'

Zain turned to Sara. 'The food should be here in ten minutes. The concierge will send it up—it's paid for. I am going out. There is a swipe card in the bowl on the console near the door, in case you need it. The Wi-Fi password is on the post-it on the fridge.'

He said all this while walking up the stairs to his room, checking messages on his phone.

Sara suddenly found herself alone on the lower floor. She looked around with her hands on her hips, took a deep breath and poured herself some hot water. Taking the Post-it with the Wi-Fi password on it, Sara walked into the study and shut the door.

About half an hour later, she heard the front door open and shut. She could hear Zain's deep voice as he spoke on his phone as he left.

It was seven in the evening. Sara returned to the living room area and found some boxes of food on the kitchen breakfast nook, realising they must have been delivered as Zain was leaving the apartment. She was famished, and so was delighted to find little boxes of rice and Kung Pao chicken and a Thai salad. She smiled, found a plate, took her food and went to sit outside and watch the city from the 30th floor.

[12]

Damn! Not again! Buzz… buzz…

Zain poked his hand out from under the covers and reached for the alarm. It wasn't on. Bloody hell!

He felt around a little more and found his phone, without even opening his eyes, 'What?' he barked into his phone.

'Zain, not what, but who! What is wrong with you?'

'*Daadijaan*,' groaned Zain, 'today is Sunday,' and opened one eye to check the time, 'it is 8 am.'

'Yes, so? I have been up since 5 am, have read my *namaaz*, walked in the garden, and have had my morning cup of tea with your *Ammi* and *Baba*. Even the twins are awake. Only that Saif is still asleep!'

'Okay, okay, I am up. What is it, *Daadijaan*?'

'I called you a hundred times yesterday and you didn't even answer my calls—such bad manners!'

'*Daadijaan*, it wouldn't occur to you that perhaps I don't want to talk.'

'Why wouldn't you want to talk to me? What have I done?'

'What have you done? Yes, what have you done, *Daadijaan*? I will leave that question for you to answer for yourself.'

'*Accha chodo*, let it be. Where is Sara?'

'How would I know?'

'I want to speak to her.'

'So call on her number, I know you have it.'

'I did, but she isn't picking my calls either. Maybe her phone isn't working. Give her the phone. I need to speak to her.'

Zain closed his eyes, shaking his head, '*Daadijaan*, I'm still in bed. When I do finally wake up properly, I shall pass on your message. *Allah hafiz.*'

'Zain. Zain. Zain!'

Zain could hear her call out his name in frustration as he disconnected the call.

He closed his eyes and tried to go back to sleep. He had come home quite late. They had actually wound up by midnight, but then he had gone to drop Leyla and gone upstairs for coffee, and... Zain smiled a little. He could do with a little more sleep.

Five minutes later, Zain got out of bed, cursing *Daadijaan*. He wasn't getting any sleep. Maybe he should head to the gym or go for a run, or get himself some coffee.

Zain padded towards the stairs and stopped halfway down. Standing in the middle of the living room on one leg, with her hands stretched towards the ceiling, eyes closed, was Sara.

He came down a few more stairs and could see her side profile, which wasn't a very good idea, as his eyes immediately focussed on her lips. They were semi-parted as she breathed out of her mouth and breathed in through her nose in a rhythmic pattern. Zain stood there looking at her. She wasn't very tall—about five feet three inches. She just about came up to his shoulders.

She was curvy. He could see her curves even through her loose yellow T-shirt and blue and white tights, which showed off her shapely legs. They weren't muscular or bony. As her hands stretched above her head, her T-shirt rode up as well and he could see a hint of skin near the waist band. Clearly she didn't have the washboard abs he was used to seeing in the women he dated. He could see a little tummy poking out, the hint of a belly button.

He shook his head, trying to get her out of it, as he walked towards the kitchen counter to turn on the coffee machine. As he waited for his coffee, his gaze went back to her. She had now brought her arms down and was standing straight with her hands folded in a namaste pose, continuing with her breathing. She had tied her hair into a high ponytail and few strands had escaped and were curling up at her nape. He could see the back of her neck—it was slim and straight, her shoulders narrow.

The whistle of the coffee machine went off just then, breaking his trance. He quickly turned away and busied himself getting his mug and pouring his coffee. When he turned back, he found she had finished her yoga and was rolling up her mat, turning towards him.

'Good morning,' she said quietly, before she walked into the study.

She returned five minutes later, her face damp. Clearly, she had splashed her face with water. The tendrils of her hair were also slightly wet. Her face looked as if it had been scrubbed clean, except for a few traces of *kaajal* in her eyes. He hadn't seen such a fresh face in years. He was trying to avoid looking at her lips.

Zain raised his mug to her asking if she wanted a cup. Sara shook her head, 'I am not much of a coffee drinker; I prefer tea.'

He pushed himself away from the counter and went to rummage in the cupboard above the fridge and brought out a gift-wrapped box, 'This was a gift from some time back—never been opened. Feel free.' He put the box in front of her.

Sara's eyes lit up. She examined the box. It was a fancy box of different kinds of fruit teas, lemon, raspberry, mint, strawberry, blackcurrant and what not—not exactly what she was looking for, but it was better than nothing. Selecting a lemon tea sachet, Sara poured herself some hot water and dipped her tea bag.

Zain helped himself to some cereal and milk and a banana. Sara watched him, wondering if it would be rude to ask if she could eat something else. Then thought she had better not. She helped herself to a banana and an apple, and sat eating both quietly.

Zain was busy on his phone and then took his food out to the deck, leaving Sara alone inside.

Sara went into the study and took out her laptop and decided to work on an assignment, and that kept her busy till the afternoon.

When she came out of her room, she could hear Zain on the phone upstairs, he was working. She wanted to have a shower, but realised she couldn't while he was home, so she went to the fridge and took out the leftovers from last night's dinner and fixed herself a plate of food. While she was eating, she saw Zain come down the stairs still on his phone. He headed towards the door, and then he was gone.

She breathed a sigh of relief! She took her plate of food to sit in front of the TV and ate quietly while flipping channels.

It was quite late by the time Zain returned. The place was all quiet. He headed to the bar to fix himself a drink. He had had a tough day, and had spent most of it- troubleshooting. He realised he hadn't had anything to eat since lunch which had been a sandwich in between calls. Picking up his glass he headed to the kitchen to see if he could make himself an egg and some toast, he was too tired to do more than that. He had just opened the fridge door, when he heard a soft voice, 'Are you hungry?'

He turned around to find Sara, her hair tousled, standing in front of him in a loose night dress. He had seen his sisters wear these when they were kids. His mom used to call them 'nighties'.

He heard her repeat her question, 'Are you hungry? Should I fix you something?'

'No, no. As in, yes, I am hungry, but I can fix myself some eggs.'

Sara moved towards the kitchen, slid between him and the fridge door which was still ajar, took out two eggs, the butter and the bread and moved towards the hob and went about organising herself.

Zain was left with nothing to do but shut the fridge door and sit down at the breakfast counter watching her as she busied herself, whisking the eggs, chopping a little onion, a little green chilly (green chilly—he didn't even know he had them in his kitchen!) popping the toast into the toaster... soon he had a delicious-looking omelette, white with bits of brown and green which were the caramelised onion and green chillies shining through and two golden slices of toast in front of him. While he looked down at his plate, she went about setting a vessel with water in it to boil, adding milk and some things, he didn't even know he owned, into it, and brought two mugs out.

He was famished and his mouth was watering, so he ate quietly, wolfing down the omelette and toast, washing it down with his whiskey. He hadn't had such good eggs in a while. Soon, he could smell cardamom and milk and tea. Sara put a mug of a frothing tea in front of him. The mug smelt like the stuff *Daadijaan* brewed. He remembered how his brothers and sisters would call it *Daadijaan's* witches' brew. It was magic and even his mother couldn't make such a delectable cup of tea, or chai, as *Daadijaan* called it.

Sara sat along the counter as he ate and sipped on her chai. She had been bored and was in desperate need of a proper cup of chai. So, she had bathed and slipped out with her swipe card and a little shopping bag. She had made friends with Max, the concierge, who told her of a small grocery store down the road that would be open. She was delighted to find the store was owned by a Mr Patel, who was thrilled to serve her and helped her pick small quantities of *masalas*, *daals*, rice and some vegetables, and yes, two small bags of Darjeeling and *masala chai*.

She had picked up a roll from his store for herself for dinner, which she had eaten earlier and planned to cook the next day. She was craving for some good home-cooked food.

Sara loved to cook; it was something she had learnt from *Sadaf Khala*, their cook and housekeeper. Whenever she was back from boarding school, everyone would usually be busy, so she would spend most of her time with *Khala* and would listen to her stories and help her in the kitchen. She had also learnt the basics of home economics in school. She hated it—all the sewing and cleaning and everything—all except the cooking. That she loved! She was the laughing stock of the family, for she had chosen to study SUPW (what was called Socially Useful and Productive Work in the curriculum and was offered to only girls' schools, and therefore, was seen as regressive), instead of computers, and her sisters and cousins had always made fun of her for that.

Watching Zain eating his eggs and toast, Sara smiled. Feeding someone always brought a smile to her face and it had made her popular in her dorm as well. Her dorm mates would love to drop in for her special *chai* and whatever she could manage on the small hot plate in her room.

Once he was done, Zain looked up from his food. He had been famished!

'Where did you get the onions and chillies?'

'From Mr Patel's store down the road.'

Huh? Zain looked at her in amazement. He had lived here for over three years and hadn't even once stepped into a store anywhere in the vicinity! This part of town hardly had any such stores, only luxury brands and upmarket fashionable stores.

Sara was chatting about how Max, the concierge, had directed her to the store, and how Mr Patel had been very helpful.

Zain reached for the mug that she had placed before him. The aroma from it was very alluring.

He looked at her delicate hands warming around her own mug, his gaze moving up towards her face. He stopped himself just in time!

Zain stood up, 'Thank you for this! You needn't have gone to the store. Next time, order on Amazon. I will add you to my card.' He put his plate in the sink, saying he would wash it tomorrow, took his cup of tea and walked upstairs to his room.

Sara, left alone in the kitchen, sighed. She quickly washed the dishes and put them out to dry. She needed to learn how to use the dishwasher and made a note of it in her mind. She switched off the lights and went into the study.

Zain was upstairs on his deck; he could see her moving about in the kitchen. He watched her go into her room and turn the lights off. He then turned to look out, sipping his chai.

[13]

Days passed like this; Zain was super busy with work. In the mornings, he would either come down to find her doing yoga in the living room or curled up in her blanket on the sofa instead of the bed in the study. He was tempted to get a proper new bed for the study knowing the pull out must be hard and uncomfortable, but, he kept telling himself, this was a temporary arrangement and that is how it should be.

Most of the days, he avoided being at home, buried himself at work, worked late if he wasn't meeting friends, and came home usually after he knew she would be asleep. Every night though, he would find a mug of *chai* on the counter for him covered with a saucer and a note which read 'Heat'. He would find some food cooked and kept in the fridge which he helped himself to as well occasionally, when he was exhausted. This was becoming a habit and he didn't like it.

But, yes, he was trying his best not to see her.

He figured she was going into work at the MET, where she was interning for the project she had been assigned, as he would occasionally find her sitting in the study working on something or sitting in the living room surrounded by books. Her books were all serious books on art and painters. Occasionally, he would spot a painting on the cover of one of the books she would leave on the coffee table which he would recognise. He wasn't into art at all, but he did know some of the great painters and their famous works. On the whole, Zain and Sara had almost no conversation with each other.

Their Whatsapp messages were also just business, 'Cleaning Lady coming today' or 'Out of town for two days' or 'At the library—will be late' or 'At the museum— will be late'. No responses. No communication. Except for the blue ticks which indicated that the message had been read.

One evening, Sara had had a long day at the museum and then had worked on her assignment for many hours. She was tired and her eyes hurt. Zain was out of town and most probably would be back later in the week. Sara stood up from her place on the coffee table where she was working, stretched her back, her neck muscles hurt as did her eyes and head. Maybe a hot shower and some sleep would help. She went to the study and picked up her night clothes. She looked towards the pull-out bed and grimaced. Perhaps she should sleep on the couch, it was at least better than that bed! She walked upstairs to Zain's room to shower. It was bliss! After ten minutes, she felt better. Changing into her night clothes and rubbing a towel over her hair, she came out of the bath and stood in front of the bed. It looked so inviting. Her legs automatically moved towards the bed and she sat down. It was soft… running her hands over the comforter on top, she relished the velvety feel… maybe just for ten minutes… her mind told her… anyway Zain isn't in town, he wouldn't know.

She lay down and took a deep breath, a little smile and her eyes closed. Just ten minutes.

It was very late at night, actually almost 2:00 am, was what his watch showed him. He had taken the red eye from London right after two days of marathon meetings, instead of spending the night and taking the flight the next day. He needed to be in office tomorrow in New York. He wanted to get back, wanted his own bed. And he needed a cup of chai.

He entered the apartment and found that everything was dark and quiet. He walked like a zombie to the kitchen counter, hoping to find a cup of *chai* there waiting for him. But naturally, it wasn't, he wasn't supposed to be home tonight.

Damn! His head was splitting and his eyes were almost shutting. He had fallen asleep in the cab back home as well. He was exhausted and might just about manage to reach his bed—at least one of the things he needed could be attained.

Zain walked upstairs, his room was all dark as well, he could see the silhouette of the bed, and wondered whether he should change, decided against it, yanking off his tie and throwing his jacket on the chair, he slipped off his shoes and crawled into his bed, his eyes already shut.

Buzz... buzz... 'Damn!' muttered Zain, switching off his phone with his eyes still closed. He was very comfortable and there was no way he was waking up. He hadn't slept this well in sometime, and his bed felt just right, soft, warm and fruity.

Fruity?! Zain froze. He opened one eye and looked down—there was a little face nestled into the crook of his neck and his arm was around a soft shoulder and arm. He opened both his eyes—he hadn't been this close to her face. Her lips... were an inch away from his. He realised their legs were entwined and she fit in perfectly. He was just so comfortable.

This felt perfect. BUT it wasn't perfect! It was not how it was supposed to be! This was not what he wanted…

He could move away immediately, and she would awaken. Or he could wait for her to wake up by herself. While he was thinking of what to do, he felt her stir and then suddenly her breathing stopped. She had woken up!

'Oh God!' Sara jumped up. But instead of making a clean break, she further entangled herself in the sheets and Zain's arms and legs. How did this happen?

'Relax! Relax! I just woke up as well. What are you doing here? This is my bed not yours.'

'I…I… was exhausted last night and after a shower, just sat down for a few minutes. I must have dozed off. I am sorry, I didn't know you were going to be back. I would never have… I am really sorry…' Sara blubbered with panic written all over her face.

'I said, relax! I didn't know I would be back myself, I was exhausted. Came home and crashed, didn't realise you were here. So just relax!'

Sara was finally out of the bed and picked up her discarded clothes from the night before and ran down the stairs to the study.

How did this happen? She felt like kicking herself. She'd said ten minutes. How could she not have woken up? Changing into fresh clothes and organising herself quickly, Sara picked up her satchel, slid her laptop into her bag, grabbed her swipe card and phone and headed out of the apartment. She had a lot of work to do and a lot on her mind. She needed to get away—she could not face him. This was not his fault—she wasn't supposed to be there.

Zain was watching her frantically move round downstairs from his sit out. He had to give her time. He had gotten out of bed after a while as well, the bed had gone cold and didn't feel the same anymore. Splashing his face with cold water hadn't helped. Maybe a bit of cold morning air was needed. It took a bit of time for her to leave, he heard the door ping shut; took a deep breath and then went downstairs, fixed himself some coffee and sat down with it. He needed to clear his head. Taking out his phone, he realised it was still switched off. Swiping it to life, Zain saw a hundred messages from work, and a few missed calls from his father, *Daadijaan* (rolled his eyes) and Walid uncle in India.

He clicked on the last number and dialled in.

'*Salamaleikum* Walid Uncle!'

'*Walaikum assalam*, Zain *beta*! Sorry, did I call too early?'

Zain smirked off late; everyone was making it a habit to call 'too early'.

'No, no, my phone had lost power. Is everything alright?'

'Yes, yes, I have been trying to get through to Sara since last evening, but she wasn't answering her phone. And now her number is coming unreachable, so I got a little worried.'

'I am not sure uncle; I wasn't in town last evening, got back very late. I think she has left for the museum this morning, and maybe in the library now, where the phones don't work. Please don't worry—she is fine. I will ask her to call you.'

'Zain, *beta*, thank you, once again! We are indebted... and would never have put you through such an inconvenience.'

Assuring Sara's father it was alright, he hung up.

One done! Did he want to speak to *Daadijaan*? No.

Zain quickly spoke to his father; thankfully it was about work and nothing else. And he found a message from Leyla wanting to meet tonight. Maybe he would... he needed a distraction—Leyla would be perfect!

[14]

Zain picked up Leyla in the evening. The two of them had been at university together; had dated on and off; had a great time together, but were very clear about it being casual—no strings attached. Leyla was a merchandiser and belonged to a mixed family. Her Dad was Pakistani and mom was a third generation American. Successful and competitive, she was very clear about what she wanted and that worked very well for Zain. He too was successful, competitive and didn't want any strings attached.

Due to her work with fashion, Leyla was always very well turned out, reed thin to ensure everything she wore looked good, her face was always made up perfectly, she knew when to smile and when to say what—and—was very good in bed.

The two of them headed to a club to meet other friends. A rocking party was already on. This was what Zain needed—to get his mind back on track. It was loud in there; it usually was, but tonight it seemed extra loud. Everyone was laughing and trying to out shout the other. Zain settled into the corner of the table, nursed his drink and pasted a smile on his face trying to listen in on the conversation—he had no idea what they were talking about. They seemed to be celebrating something. A round of drinks arrived. They were celebrating a big deal that Leyla had done. Leyla stood up to make a toast to herself, raised her glass and her dress rode up, showing her navel. He could see each rib and how taut her skin was. Not soft…

His eyes rode up to her face. Her face was shiny with a glitter bronzer, her eyes smoky with eye shadow and eye lashes unnaturally long and curled. Her lips were covered in a dark gloss. He realised he didn't really know how they looked without lipstick… and he didn't want to know either.

Leyla sat down and curled up next to him, cooing in his ear. He could hardly hear her. He needed to get out. Grabbing Leyla's hand, Zain whispered in her ear, 'Let's go to my place.' Leyla looked at his face and smiled and winked. And soon they left. Taking Leyla home to his place was Zain's way of proving to himself that Sara being at his place and his attraction towards her was nothing of any consequence.

Zain let Leyla all over himself at the back of the cab as the driver navigated them towards his apartment. As they fell into the apartment, they started shedding their clothes and just about made their way upstairs. Leyla pushed Zain back onto the bed. The minute his body touched the bed, he froze. The morning came rushing back to him. He could still see her face next to his, her lips; feel her breath on his arm and her soft body curled up next to his. He could still smell her fruity body spray. He shut his eyes tight and suddenly realised he had Leyla climbing over him. He reached out to hold her, but instead, he held her away. Leyla froze. What was happening?

'Zain?'

'I can't do it.'

'Zain, what the fuck?'

Raising her voice, she repeated herself.

'Leyla, I am sorry.'

She rolled off him, still glaring at him—clearly pissed.

'Leyla,' Zain said a little while later, 'you can't spend the night.'

'What? Why?'

'Just, I don't feel well now. Please, I am sorry.'

Leyla's glare could have burnt him, but he got off the bed and walked over to his door. His clothes were all out of place, and his hair all tousled.

'Fuck you!' Leyla muttered. And then repeated herself louder, 'FUCK YOU!'

Grabbing her top and shoes, Leyla stormed out of Zain's room picking up her scarf from the stairs and her coat from near the main door. She banged the front door shut. Hearing the door slam, Zain finally took a deep breath.

He closed his door shut and slammed his fist against the wall—SHIT!

A cold shower was what he needed and so headed to his bathroom and locked himself in.

Twenty minutes of tossing and turning in bed were enough for Zain. He couldn't sleep. He sat up and looked out of his window. Maybe a drink would help, maybe some chai. No, he just needed to sleep, like he did last night.

Zain stood up abruptly, ran his hand through his still damp hair, pulled on a T-shirt over his tracks and walked down the stairs.

He instinctively walked past the kitchen counter, hoping to find a cup of *chai* waiting for him, but there wasn't. He did find the PostIt next to it, but it was blank. Maybe she changed her mind.

He stood there and fingered the little PostIt, deep in thought. Crumpling the piece of paper, he moved towards the study with a determined look on his face. This was the only way...

[15]

Sara had been lying awake in her uncomfortable bed in the Study when she heard the ping of the elevator. She had to speak to Zain and apologise... it wasn't right!

She quietly got out of bed and walked into the living area in the dark, still hidden by the tall plant in the corner, she saw Zain and a woman stumble in. Holding her breath, she stayed hidden. She could see Zain and the woman all over each other, stripping off their layers, they just about managed to close the front door and crawled up the stairs, stuck to each other as though they couldn't get enough... she could hear them upstairs...

Tears in her eyes, she turned around and went back into her room and covered her ears with her hands and dove beneath the covers as deep as she could bury herself.

Why not? She told herself. Yes, why not? Why should he not have a girlfriend, why shouldn't he bring her home... to his home... how did it matter whether she was there or not.... What were they to each other? She was just someone staying at his house while she did her work in New York, he hadn't wanted her to be there, she was forcefully dumped on him this time just like she had been those many years ago... neither of them had a choice...

So yes, why shouldn't he...?

She had earlier in the night, before going to bed, thought about making him a cup of *chai* and leaving it for him like she usually did... but thought against it as she was about to write the Post-it, and had poured the tea down the kitchen drain and had gone to bed. She was embarrassed about last night, and leaving him a cup of *chai* would have been so predictable... No...she would speak to him and apologise. Face-to-face...

Then, she heard him enter the house and then...

Yes, why not? Why was she getting upset?

Silently curled up in bed, Sara tried to calm her breathing... then she heard the girl raise her voice... and could hear her heels clicking down the stairs and then after a few seconds, she heard the front door slam...

Huh? Sara removed the blanket from her face and lay silently... shutting her eyes, trying to sleep. How did it matter to her?

After sometime she thought she heard the door to the study open slowly and she heard or sensed... someone entered.... It had to be Zain... she lay still... she could sense him standing near her bed... then suddenly she felt herself being lifted... blanket et al...

What? Stunned... she opened her eyes in shock and looked up at Zain... a face that was now so familiar. He had on his trademark grim expression, but his eyes bore into her.

'Don't say a word,' he said. He carried her out of the study, and up the stairs... taking them two at a time.

Sara had a look of total confusion in her eyes... she held on to his neck... her fingers clutching his shoulder.... What was he doing?

They had reached his room and he was still carrying her. She looked at the bed and then up at him... and parted her lips hoping to have the courage to ask him...

When... 'Shhh!!' His face was very close to hers. Even in the dimly lit room, she could see his eyes boring into hers, 'Please don't say a thing... I am not going to do anything... Shhh... I just need you to sleep in the bed next to me... Please...'

Sara's eyes were still confused, her lips still parted, she licked her lips in her anxiety...and saw Zain close his eyes as she did that.

He wanted her to sleep next to him... she repeated his words in her head... huh?

But, much to her dismay, she found herself gently nodding and agreeing to Zain's request. She was still confused.... Why had she agreed? She should be petrified... but then realised... she was confused... but not scared or afraid... she trusted him!

Zain felt relieved when he saw her nod. He had almost lost control when he saw her lick her lips, and clutched her even firmly. Now he gently lowered her onto his bed, removed her blanket and tucked her into his own. Walking around to his side, he got in, glancing at her. She was laying stiffly on her side, still a little uncertain...

He slid under the covers and moved closer to her... moving one arm around her, he drew her close, pulled her back towards him and snuggled in. She could feel his breath around her nape... it was strangely comforting and calming...

Slowly she felt her own breathing settle and realised he had actually fallen asleep. She felt her own eyelids grow heavy and soon was asleep, unknowingly smiling as she did. Not knowing that Zain had a similar expression on his sleeping face as well.

Buzzzz!!! Buzzz!!!! Zain picked up his phone from the bedside table and threw it to the other side of the room, where it landed with a thud. He moved his arm back to where it had been resting... on Sara's tummy, holding her close. His other arm was under her head and her hair was spread all over his pillow. Her head was turned the other way giving him a clear view of her slender nape and the hand on her tummy rose and fell as she slept. She was still asleep... but he was wide awake... which was a good thing... he needed to take stock of the situation.

He had practically carried her to his bed and she had agreed. They had shared a bed and slept... that was it... for now.

He suddenly had a flashback of what all had happened the previous night between him and Leyla, mentally making a note of apologising to her and sending her flowers or something, after all he had led her on.

And then, there was this situation.

Sara turned her head towards him, still asleep, licking her lips as she turned. Zain closed his eyes.... This was sheer torture... and he still hadn't fathomed why she was affecting him this much. He had seen many women before this, so why?

He suddenly felt her breathing stop and opened his eyes to find her big eyes wide open and looking at him in confusion.

He could see the events of last night flash across her eyes... she almost darted from the bed... and he had to hold her from running...

'Relax!... Shh! Relax... ' He held her close, breathing in the fruity fragrance around her nape. Slowly he felt her breathing settled and looked at her and whispered, 'Good morning...'

Before she could say anything... Buzzzz!!! Buzzzz!!! The phone didn't seem to be very close, but was buzzing somewhere...

The two of them lay there quietly, waiting for it to stop. But, it didn't...

Zain finally muttered, 'I think I need to get it...'

Slowly moving away from her, disentangling himself from the sheets and covers, Zain, tried to figure out where he had thrown his phone. It had fallen behind the standing lamp at the end of the room. Retrieving it, he saw Sara's father's name flash on the screen. Zain turned towards the bed and mouthed... your *Abba*...

Sara almost died! She was anyway still in a state of shock and confusion, and now she felt her heart stop beating... she looked at Zain anxiously...

She saw him turn away from her, to give her some time to settle herself, and spoke into the phone.

'Good morning, Uncle!'

'Good morning, Zain *beta*! How are you? Sorry again to call you this early, we keep forgetting the time difference...'

'It is alright uncle...'

'You see, again that careless girl, Sara, isn't answering her phone.... Today is Saturday morning for you, she couldn't be at the museum or library.... We called her many times, but there was no response...' Sara's father gushed in embarrassment for disturbing Zain early in the morning.

He continued, 'Actually, I am sure you know, but it is her birthday today... and we wanted to wish her. But that silly girl isn't picking up her phone...'

Zain froze.

Her birthday? He turned towards her and saw her quietly getting out of bed, picking up her blanket and moving towards the door...

'Zain...?'

'Yes... Uncle, she must be asleep or in the washroom,' he responded slowly, 'I will have her call you in a bit.'

'Okay *beta... Allah Hafiz!*'

Sara had left and Zain was left standing in the middle of his room. It was her birthday... and then it also meant...

Buzzz... Buzz... Zain clenched his phone... about to throw it against the wall, when he saw *Daadijaan's* name flash on the screen. Taking a deep breath, he took the call.

'Finally, Zain... this is the height of bad manners! I have been calling you for the past few days and you have been avoiding my calls.' He heard an authoritative voice bellow through his phone.

'*Salam Walaikum Daadijaan...*'

'Walaikum assalam... Anyway, I didn't want to talk to you! I wanted to talk to Sara and she isn't answering her phone. Where is she? Why isn't she answering her phone? What could she be doing at this time of the morning... it is Saturday... I..'

'Daadijaan,' Zain interrupted her monologue, 'She must have been away from her phone... perhaps speaking to her family in India. You could call her now!'

Zain abruptly disconnected his phone...

Taking a deep breath, he went into his bathroom and slammed the door shut.

An hour later, Zain emerged, bathed, shaved and ready to face the day... her birthday... and...

As he came down the stairs, he saw her busy in the kitchen, organising breakfast-eggs and toast... for one.... This got his antennae up. Was she going somewhere...?

He started making his coffee, watching her from the corner of his eye.

He found Sara moving away from the kitchen. She had used the time he was changing to do the same herself. Dressed in a white sweatshirt and a pair of jeans, hair loose around her nape, framing her face, eyes lined with kohl which was normal and her lips bare... she wrapped her crimson scarf around her neck and picked up her satchel. Clearly avoiding looking at him.

'Where are you off to?' Zain's deep voice cut through the silence in the apartment stopping her in her tracks...

'I need to go to the museum,' she replied in a soft voice.

'Today? It's Saturday, I am sure you have no classes today.'

'Uuuuhhhh... No,...I have a meeting at the museum... so I need... uhhhhh... to be there as soon as possible...' Sara stammered and responded to his question.

She tried her best to find plausible excuses to disappear from the house. She had to get away... she was still confused about the previous night...!

Zain looked at her, over the rim of his cup as he sipped his coffee. She was finding excuses... she wanted to get away.... What should he do? Call her bluff? Let her go... it was after all her birthday... and... also...

Sara didn't know which way to look... she stood with her back to him... about to head out towards the door...

'Sara, I could meet you for lunch... I am free today.' Zain was surprised to hear himself say this as he saw her head towards the door.

This made her freeze... She turned around and looked at him, 'Listen... we may have slept together, but it means nothing... you don't owe me anything.'

'Correction,' Zain's deep voice cut across the distance between them, 'we didn't sleep together, but slept next to each other. There is a huge difference and thank you for letting me know that I owe you nothing...'

'I wanted to let you know that I was going to be home today, so if you did come home...we could have lunch together...' He continued looking straight at her.

'I... am not sure...' she hesitated.

'Okay, let me know…I am here today…' He curtly responded and went back to looking at his phone.

'Okay… I need to go…' saying this, Sara quickly turned around and headed out of the door.

Left alone in the apartment, Zain sat quietly eating the plate of food she had set before him. Heading out to the deck with his coffee, he walked up to the bench where he sat and nursed his coffee. What happened last night? In a way it had changed everything. His actions had changed the dynamics of everything and she didn't seem to have any objection last night. Though her reaction this morning was strange. He wasn't surprised, he had actually expected this confusion not only for her, but also for him.

What was it about Sara that was getting to him…? Did he like her?… He didn't know.

Did he lust for her… Yes!

Did he need her… Yes!

Was this against what he had planned for himself? Yes!! Most definitely, Yes!!

There was no way he was going to concede defeat. He had been forced into this marriage years ago and it needed to end.

But, today was her birthday… she didn't know he knew… he needn't tell her he knew.

The only problem was that he knew if it was her birthday…. It meant it was also the anniversary of their *Nikaah* and he was sure that was an event both of them wanted to forget.

Anyway, now she was gone and he was here alone!

Moving back indoors, he looked at his phone. There were missed calls from Leyla. Yes, she deserved an explanation. Sighing deeply and grimacing at the same time, Zain picked up his phone to speak to Leyla, apologising about how he had suddenly felt unwell and that he had felt it wasn't right to lead her on. So, he had stopped her right at the beginning.

She must have been busy with work, as she agreed without much persuasion. Zain then settled in with his own work and spent the entire morning working the phones and sorting out minor problems in their offices and factories in Africa, where the employees worked Saturdays as well.

His stomach started to growl at around 2 pm. He needed to eat lunch. Stretching and loosening his muscles, Zain was just about to head towards the kitchen, when he heard the swipe card ping and the door open. Sara stood on the other side and gingerly entered the apartment. As she reached the main foyer, she cautiously removed her jacket and went towards the living area. As she moved towards the study, she saw Zain sitting in the living room working on his laptop, she dropped her bag off in her room and moved towards the kitchen. Fixing the vessel with water and adding the cardamom and milk and letting the mix boil. He watched her brew the tea and sniffed the fragrance of the cardamom as it filled the air. It was raining outside and this was exactly what he needed.

Watching her set a cup before him, his gaze followed her to the couch on the far side, near the windows overlooking Central Park. Sipping his *chai*, he watched her across the rim of his mug.

Finishing his *chai*, Zain stood up. 'Lunch?' His deep voice always seemed to startle her.

Sara looked up and found him standing right in front of her. 'Umm.... No, I am not hungry, I grabbed a sandwich at the museum.... Thank you.'

Zain looked at her and then abruptly turned around, grabbed his jacket and walked out of the apartment. As he went down the elevator, he thought to himself... maybe this was best. They needed to avoid each other. He had made up his mind...

Sara heaved a sigh of relief as Zain left. This was really going to be difficult. She needed to avoid him. She went into the study and shut the door determined to not come out at all.

[16]

Zain walked around Central Park trying to sort out his head. He needed to distance himself from Sara, which was going to be difficult as they lived in the same house. He would need to plan a lot of travel and work while she was here in New York, perhaps a trip back home to see his parents and speak to his Dad about working on the annulment as well, so that this entire chapter could get some closure was what was needed. Yes, that was more like a plan.

On his way home Zain walked past many high street stores that dotted the neighbourhood. His eye caught the reflection of something shining in a window. He was in front of Tiffany's. There was a lot of stuff glittering at him and he spotted a delicate chain with an array of pendants that could be strung on. It would look perfect... No! No! Zain caught himself in time and walked briskly ahead.

Quietly entering the apartment, he glanced around. The door to the study was firmly shut. Picking up his laptop from the living room coffee table, he headed upstairs to his

room and shut the door firmly as well.

He shut out all other thoughts and buried himself in work, this was the best way forward. At around 7 in the evening, he finally got up and realised he needed to eat and get himself a drink. Walking downstairs, he realised the study door was still shut. The doorbell pinged, his pizza must have arrived.

He fixed himself a stiff drink and took the pizza out to the deck to eat and get some fresh air. He always loved to sit out in the evening, the glittering lights and the cool breeze always calmed him. Taking a sip of his drink, he realised Sara would not have eaten anything either... shaking his head, forgetting it... let her figure it out... he had best avoid it...

Taking another sip, he looked out into the sky which looked like a painting. Shutting his eyes, he shook his head. He was now comparing his view to art, Good lord!! He wasn't like this. Damn it! She had gotten under his skin...

His third sip of the golden liquid made him stand up, put his glass down and walk back inside. He banged on the study door...

Sara opened the door with a startled expression on her face...

'Dinner?' He asked her, raising an eyebrow.

When Sara finally found her voice. She vehemently shook her head and said that she wasn't hungry. She turned to shut the door again, when Zain pushed it open again...

'Stop it! Yes, we need to avoid each other, but you also need to eat. So act mature and not like a child.... After all, you are a year older today.

Sara looked up at him stunned. She stood with her mouth open... and her eyes became as big as saucers... Zain... bit his lips and muttered under his breath. Shit! He hadn't wanted to mention it.

Zain stood to the side to allow her to pass him.

'Out on the deck... I ordered pizza. Do you want something to drink?'

Sara shook her head as she slowly walked to the deck. She eyed the box of pizza and saw his glass of whiskey beside it. He hadn't started to eat. Sara sat down on one of the chairs at the table and looked out. How had he known it was her birthday? Did he remember what else was today?

Her thoughts were broken when he placed a glass of red wine in front of her and sat down in the chair next to her. He opened the box of pizza and raised his glass, 'Happy Birthday!'

Gulping slowly, she picked up the wine glass in front of her and tried to smile, 'Thank you!'

They sat there in silence, sipping their drink and nibbling on the pizza.

Strains of music started to be heard in the background. There was someone listening to loud music somewhere close by. It was really nice jazz. The music from the piano and saxophone was beautiful. They sat in silence. It was quite peaceful...

'How did you know?' Sara suddenly asked him.

Zain turned and looked at her, 'I didn't... your father told me this morning and then so did *Daadijaan*. Did you speak to them? They called me as your phone was not reachable. It must have been downstairs in the morning, when they called.'

Sara shook her head, 'No... I messaged them, and didn't feel like talking!'

Zain looked at her over the rim of his glass. She was looking straight ahead, wringing her hands on her lap and biting her lips.

Zain shut his eyes and took a deep breath to calm himself...

Placing his glass on the table, he picked up his phone and placed a video call to Sara's father.

'Hello... Walid uncle... *Salamaleikum*...'

Sara looked towards him, her eyes flashing... What was he doing?

'Zain *beta... walaiekum asalam...* is everything alright... so early in the morning?' she could hear the worried voice of her father at the other end.

'Yes, all okay! I thought you would like to speak to Sara, since you didn't earlier.'

'Yes.. Yes... we didn't manage...'

Zain turned his phone towards Sara...

'Sara... Happy birthday *beta*... we have been trying to speak to you since morning...'

'Thank you *Abba*! Yes I know...' Sara's eyes welled with tears.

Zain sat back and watched her. He could see her smiling and pushing back her tears as the rest of her family also came into the frame, her mother and her sister. Everyone was talking at the same time... and Sara was trying to answer all their questions...

He stood up and quietly cleared the table of the pizza box and her glass and went inside, giving her the privacy she needed.

Ten minutes later, Sara came back inside and handed him his phone, 'Thank you.. for the dinner and wine and the call... Good night!'

Sara turned around and went back to the study and shut the door, without turning back even once.

Zain tossed and turned in his bed... Damn! He finally looked at his phone... it flashed at 2 am... and he hadn't been able to sleep a wink...

He got out of bed and paced the room. Maybe he needed a drink. Walking downstairs, he headed towards his bar. When suddenly he spotted her sitting in a corner of the living room, wrapped in her blanket.

Walking slowly towards her, 'Sara?'

Sara looked startled as soon as she heard her name, 'Zain..?'

'Why are you up?' He asked her gently.

'I couldn't sleep...' she said softly, looking at him.

He could see the tiredness in her eyes, she must have spent the entire day in front of her computer like him. He was in a similar state, if he didn't get some sleep tonight he would be useless tomorrow and he had a row of important meetings lined up.

Zain instinctively moved forward and picked Sara up, like he had the night before and carried her upstairs to his room... there was no other way out.

And like before, she didn't resist.

They were both asleep in five minutes flat, curled up against each other.

The next morning, Sara woke up to find herself alone in Zain's bed. Checking the bedside clock she saw it was 10 am! She must have slept in, and a quick glance around the room indicated that Zain had left for work, he usually did by 9.

Reluctantly getting out of bed, Sara padded downstairs and put the kettle on to boil. She could smell Zain's coffee in the kitchen. Quickly getting ready, Sara also left for the museum.

Her phone buzzed as she walked out of the apartment… glancing at the screen, she saw she had a message from *Daadijaan* asking how she had spent her birthday. She smiled and responded with a picture of pizza and a glass of wine. With a smile on her face, Sara headed off towards work.

She waited up till 9 at night with her dinner and then finally ate alone. Should she message and ask Zain? No… they hadn't even exchanged a word since last night. She sat reading in her room, not knowing what to do…

At around 11, she heard the front door ping, glancing towards the door, she contemplated going out to meet Zain, but decided against it. She quickly turned her light off and tried to sleep. Ten minutes later, she threw the blanket off and walked out of the room and headed towards the stairs. As she climbed up a few stairs, she found herself face to face with Zain's chest. He was on his way down…

They looked at each other for a few minutes, and then Zain stepped aside quietly to let her pass and followed her back upstairs.

Buzzz..Buzz… Zain groaned. He was going to lose his phone one of these days, on purpose.

He opened one eye and realised he was alone in bed. Checking his buzzing phone... to find it was only 7 am, he started to sit up in bed. Where was she?

'Hello?'

'*Bhai*? Not too early I hope?'

'*Saif*...? What's up?' Zain replied ignoring his brother's second question.

'*Bhai*, Mum wanted to know if you would be coming home next weekend for *Daadijaan's* birthday?'

'Oh... I forgot... Will check my schedule and let you all know... I am travelling this week already, but let me see.'

'Please try *bhai*... It is her 80th...and she is being true to form and acting like a Diva!' Saif said with a laugh.

'She has planned a big celebration for herself. We were all informed of it last evening, which is why Mom wanted me to warn you.' His brother continued.

Shaking his head and smiling, Zain replied, 'Let me organise my life and I will let you know.'

'*Bhai*... oh... one more thing... you will need to bring Sara with you as well...'

'Sara? Why?' Zain snapped..

Saif responded, 'Orders from *Daadijaan*...' and disconnected the phone.

Zain looked at his phone with irritation... then sighed deeply and shook his head...

He got out of bed and walked into his bathroom. Picking up his toothbrush, he glanced at the bright pink toothbrush next to his. Sara had started keeping some of her toiletries in his bathroom. He guessed it made life easier for her, but it definitely made life more difficult for him!

He walked downstairs, expecting to find her doing yoga, but she wasn't there. The study was empty as well. Puzzled, he looked outside on the deck... not there as well... had she left... So early?

Should he message and ask... Zain thought to himself. Then, shook his head... No... no need...

That night when he returned from work, he found the apartment all quiet. Pouring himself a drink, he rummaged through the fridge to find something to eat and found many boxes with food in them. She had cooked. Setting himself a plate of food, he went looking for her.

She wasn't in the study, nor was she on the deck. Then he saw a light on in his bedroom. Carrying his plate of food upstairs, he entered the room to find Sara curled up, asleep, in bed. He stood there and watched her for a few minutes. She looked calm and her lips kept moving, forming a smile and then straightening... as though she was dreaming.

Taking a gulp, Zain turned around and went back downstairs to finish his meal without her as a distraction. He had a bit of work to finish as well. Once he was done, he changed and slid into bed and slowly drew Sara close. She murmured something and licked her lips as she turned her face towards him, still fast asleep.

Zain watched her for a bit, his gaze kept moving towards her parted lips and then closed his eyes as well.

[17]

This pattern continued for the entire week. Neither of them would see each other in the morning. Either Sara or Zain would have already left before the other woke up. They didn't speak unless needed and didn't send any messages to each other either. It was as though they just needed each other at night. Both were uncomfortable with the situation, but neither mentioned it and this went on.

The weekend saw the two of them stay out of each other's way as well.

On the next Monday morning Sara woke up, and went about getting ready for work. She saw a message on her phone. It was from Zain.

Puzzled, she looked at it, 'Going out of town... Sunday is *Daadijaan's* 80th birthday. I will send you your ticket for Friday... will come to SF directly.'

Sara's eyes widened. She didn't know what made her more anxious: *Daadijaan's* birthday and her going to San Francisco or the fact that Zain wasn't going to be in town the entire week.

She thought about what to reply, and then typed out... 'Okay' and sent it.

Zain, read her message immediately. Staring at her one word response. He had expected her to ask some questions, but she hadn't!

He had a long week ahead filled with important meetings, many flights to catch and a lot of work to do. So he shook his head and put her out of his mind.

That night, Sara went upstairs to sleep, but wasn't able to. She tossed and turned, but couldn't.

Zain stood near the window in his hotel room in London. It was raining outside and it was 3 am... and he hadn't been able to sleep a wink. He had tried! He looked at his phone.... Was she able to sleep?

This went on for the entire week. Neither of them got much sleep, but didn't speak nor message each other. There was radio silence between them.

On Thursday, Sara saw a message from Zain. He had sent her ticket to San Francisco like he had said he would.

It was just the ticket... no message along with it.

She responded with a 'Thank you.' and she could see that he had read her response.

Sara was sitting on the deck outside his room. She had tried to sleep every night, but hadn't been able to. She felt like a zombie! She was exhausted and now would have to go to San Francisco looking like a rag.

Zain read her response and put his phone away. He raked his hands through his hair and turned to look at his reflection in the mirror. He could see a shadow under his eyes and he desperately needed a shave. He was still in London, but had flown to Paris and Berlin over the past few days as well. He would have to blame how he looked on his travel schedule and not on the fact that he had hardly been able to sleep since he had left New York. Zain had messaged Saif to pick Sara up from the airport, so he would now see her only on Friday night directly at home.

Sara landed at SFO airport and picked up her *strolley* and headed outside. She had received a message from Saif saying he would be there to pick her up. He had also politely sent a photograph of himself, so that she would be able to recognise him. Sara had met him before, but she had zero memory of anyone from that evening. She had however seen a family photograph of Zain's entire family at the apartment. It was kept in his study, her room, but it looked like it was from a few years ago.

She came out of the automatic doors to find him standing right outside. Walking towards him, she smiled and could see him respond as well. He clearly knew what she looked like. Soon they were off to the house, and a waiting *Daadijaan*.

Sara was a little nervous. She would be meeting the entire family properly for the first time. Saif was energetic and easy to chat with and kept up a friendly conversation throughout the drive. He filled her in on all those who would be there and pointed out interesting places they drove past. He seemed totally different from his brother, absolutely the opposite in fact.

Sara was a little wary of meeting Zain's mother and father. No one had made an attempt to speak with her or even meet her since that evening and even Armaan uncle had spoken to her only when she had arrived in the US. She felt they didn't want to and were opposed to what had taken place that evening, which was quite natural. All of Zain's siblings were older than her, they must have been quite upset with what had happened. Though she knew that she was not at fault, she did feel uncomfortable.

Sara loved the house immediately. As Saif swung the car into the short drive way which curved in a semicircle in front of the porch, she suddenly felt very welcome. The front porch was framed with flowers in different colours, it looked lovely. The house had a well-kept garden on all sides and it looked like each room opened out into a green patch. She immediately realised why Zain had bought that apartment in a concrete jungle like New York. Each window in his apartment overlooked the only green belt in the city. It must have reminded him of home.

Sara got out of the car and smiled at Saif, who had already taken out her bag from the boot and was waving at someone. She turned around to find *Daadijaan* and another very dignified looking lady. She looked just like she did in the photograph she had seen. That photograph with his parents and siblings was actually the only personal touch that was there in Zain's apartment. The rest of the apartment was, though, very stylish, a little impersonal. Even the colours were all white, blue, grey and black.

'*Salaam aaleikum Daadijaan, Salaamaelukum* Aunty...' Sara smiled nervously at both the women standing in front of her

'Sara... I am so happy you have come... see Jahanara... see how lovely she is... she has grown up a lot since you saw her last...'

Jahanara stiffened a little at the mention of when she had seen Sara last, but then smiled at her and asked to come inside the house. Sara nervously stepped in and instantly felt the warmth the entire place emanated. It reminded her of her home in Dehradun.

Zain walked out of the airport and got into the waiting car. He couldn't wait to get home and was looking forward to meeting his entire family... and... he shook his head... No... just them...

As he stepped into the house, Zorro, one of the family's dogs, came bounding up to him... Zain was his favourite and he clearly missed the eldest boy of the house...

'*Aaa!! Bas*... now we shall have Zain, the piper, being followed everywhere by Zorro, his faithful tail...'

'You are just jealous...' growled Zain as he stood up and smiled at his brother and took him in a bear hug. Saif took Zain's suitcase and moved towards his room, while Zain walked into the family den where he was sure to find everyone.

He was right. Shrieks and loud voices welcomed him as soon as he entered. He bent down to hug his father who was seated on his favourite chair and grinned at his sisters who were sitting on a couch chatting with him. He turned towards *Daadijaan* who was seated on another couch across from them and bent down to seek her blessings. Saif and his mom entered at the same time. Zain hugged his mom tight and kissed her forehead, he had missed her. Everyone was talking at the same time just like always.

Zain sat down next to his mother with a smile on his face, fielding all the questions everyone was throwing his way. At the same time, his eyes moved around the room as if searching for something... or someone...

Just then he got a whiff of cardamom and milk… and right on cue… Sara entered carrying a huge tray laden with a big tea pot and many empty mugs.

'*Waahhh!*… Sara… God bless you…!' *Daadijaan* spoke aloud, 'From the fragrance of the *chai* I am certain you know how to make my special brew. See Jahanara… I told you… she is a gem!!'

Sara was smiling as she put the tray down… and only then did she realise that Zain was sitting next to his mother. She froze… and stared at him… and he stared back.

'Sara *beta*, pour everyone a mug and then come and sit next to me,' *Daadijaan* spoke loudly and turned to say something to the twins, asking them to help Sara.

Sara unfroze and quickly moved to do what she had been asked to do. As she poured, the twins passed on the mugs to Saif, their father, mother and *Daadijaan*, took their own and sat back down. Sara was left with two mugs. She got up and handed Zain one and sat down with her own next to *Daadijaan*, directly opposite him.

'Wah! Sara, this cup of *chai* is as good as *Daadijaan's*…' said Saif and everyone chimed in with similar responses. Zain sipped his cup and watched Sara. She blushed as she received her praise. The family chatted on, giving Zain an opportunity to observe her quietly. He noticed that she looked a little tired and could see the faint traces of dark circles beneath her eyes. His gaze moved to her lips and he watched her talking, her lips moving as she responded to something his mother was asking her.

'*Bhai*, you look like hell…!! You must have had a tough week.' Saif suddenly spoke out above the chatter. He had been quiet, all this while.

'Yes... it has been tough... I have been travelling between London, Paris, and Berlin... long meetings... and almost no sleep.' he said these last few words looking at Sara.

Sara looked at him for a few seconds and then turned her face away, biting her lower lip as she did...

Jahaanara looking at her son's tired face said, 'Chalo then let us organise dinner. Sara has also had a long flight and must be tired as well. Anyway, *Ammijaan* has lots of plans for the weekend...' rolling her eyes at the rest of the family.

'Yes, yes! Everyone must rest, tomorrow I have planned a picnic just for us... and have asked Aslam and Feroz and their families to join us on Sunday for a barbeque...' she informed them with twinkling eyes and a broad smile on her face.

Later that night, after everyone had retired to their rooms, Zain stepped out from the shower and almost fell over Zorro... who had, as Saif predicted, attached himself to Zain and had parked himself in his room. Zain opened the door from his room that faced the garden. Zorro would need to be let out once before he settled for the night...

On this side of the house the garden was between two wings, each housing a bedroom...one was his and one was *Daadijaan's*. All other rooms were on the other side of the house.

Zain stepped outside with Zorro and looked across the small patch of grass to find Sara sitting outside *Daadijaan's* room reading under the verandah light. He stood there watching her for some time. His trance-like state was interrupted when he heard Sara talking to Zorro.

Zorro had gone over to Sara, nuzzling her near her knees and she was tickling him under his jaw and talking softly to him. He walked over and stood before them. Sara looked up to find Zain in front of her in an old round neck college T-shirt and shorts. He had bathed and his hair was still slightly damp. He still looked tired.

'Was your flight on time?'

Sara was startled by the deep voice in the silence of the night.

'Yes.. it was, thank you... How was your trip?' she replied softly, hoping their voices wouldn't wake *Daadijaan* up.

'Hectic and tiring...'

Sara stood up and walked two steps towards him. She took a bold step and raised her hand to gently touch his face.

'You look really tired... you need to sleep!' she whispered.

Zain caught his breath in his mouth and his heart stopped beating as he felt her soft hand on his face. He caught her hand and kept it on his face, bringing it slowly to his lips, but not really letting them touch.

'So do you...' he whispered back, still holding her hand near his lips, his eyes on her lips and her upturned face.

She nodded quietly and turned slightly to motion towards *Daadijaan's* room behind her.

Zain whispered, 'Don't worry about her... she always pops a sleeping pill at night and sleeps very soundly.'

Zain turned around still holding on to Sara's hand and led her to his room, Zorro followed them quietly, not making a sound. He went past them into Zain's room and settled himself down near the door on the other side.

Sara stood in the middle of the room; her hands folded in front of her. Zain had let go of her hand and turned to close the door from the garden and draw the curtains. He turned towards her and walked up to stand right in front of her. Taking both her hands in his, Zain placed them around his neck and gathered her up close.

'I need you...'

Sara moved her hands around his neck and laced her fingers into his hair. She just about reached his shoulders. His arms were cradling her from the back. She closed her eyes and rested her head on his chest. This was the first time they had hugged; it was very different from when they slept together. She could feel the difference.

'Sara, I need you...'

Sara looked up at him and nodded. Zain bent down, picked her up and carried to his bed. This bed was a little narrower than the bed in his apartment, but as they lay down they fit perfectly.

Zain held her close... his face very close to her... and his eyes were on her lips... this time he couldn't stop himself... he gently lowered his lips to hers... very gently caressing them with his...almost like a whisper and then latching on to them...and gently sucking on them...as if never wanting to let go...

Slowly he felt her kiss him back as well...the gentle kissing soon changed into passionate urgency...

He moved closer to her gently moving his hands over her breasts, cupping one through her T-shirt. All the while kissing her, his hand moved lower to her soft belly, while his knees gently nudged her legs apart. Their lips broke apart as they both needed to breathe.

Just then, suddenly, he felt her stop breathing and freezing. He sensed her getting tense and looked at her face; her stricken and panicky face made him stop...

'Zain...' she stammered.

He closed his eyes tight and took a deep breath.

'It's okay... relax... let us just sleep... both of us need to if we want to make it through tomorrow.'

Zain felt her breathing again. He moved to one side of her, turned her around with her back facing him, pulled her close and curled up behind her and whispered into her ear, 'Sleep...'

[18]

Zain entered the dining room where he found everyone settling in for a quick cup of tea and breakfast all sweaty and wet. He had gone for a run to sort out his head…

'*Aare* Zain… you went for a run? You looked exhausted last night and should have slept in…' Jahanara spoke up, the concern evident in her voice…

Everyone turned to look at him. Zain quickly glanced at the person sitting in one corner of the table next to *Daadijaan* and then moved his eyes around the table to smile at the others.

'Well! He smells and is all sweaty… Yuck! But, he does look much better than last night,' chirped up Zara.

'Yes, I agree. What secret potion did you take Zain *bhai*… please share,' Sana joined her in ragging her eldest brother.

Sara felt her face heat up and covered it with her tea cup, lowering her eyes when she heard the twins teasing comments.

'It is called sleep… a really good sleep… !!' Zain replied, acting as though he was about to sock them.

'It sure seems to have been a very sweet and magical 'sleep' *bhai*...' Saif stopped half way into his jibe...as he caught his brother's grim expression.

'What time do we leave for the picnic, *Daadijaan*? I need a shower before that...' asked Zain looking towards his grandmother.

'We have to leave by 10 am, so you have time. We are driving to a lovely place an hour and a half away and I have asked the caterers to have all the food ready by 1 pm... so we shall have enough time to enjoy the lovely area around it... and we can then drive back by early evening...' The stately lady announced for everyone's benefit and then turned to her grandson, 'Zain you must bring Sara back via the Bay... it is her first trip here... she must see the Golden Gate by sunset...'

Saif piped up. 'I can show Sara the sunset...'

'I'll take her...and anyone else who wants to join us.' cut in Zain, 'That is a good idea, *Daadijaan*!'

Sara sat quietly and listened to all the chatter around her. Her eyes on and off glancing at Zain. She turned to *Daadijaan* to thank her and found the old lady smiling at her with a knowing look on her face and so quickly averted her eyes, taking another sip of her chai.

Zain walked back to his room and headed for a shower. He glanced at his hastily made bed and stopped in his tracks.

This morning at 5am, while he was deep in sleep, he had felt someone gently patting his arm. He then heard his name being whispered very close to his ear... he slowly stirred and opened his eyes to find a set of lips right in front of him.

He moved his fingers to touch them... and heard his name again...

Zain raised his face a little and looked down at Sara, she was totally trapped under

him. Their legs were entwined and his arms were holding her close. He was holding her like one would hold a stuffed toy.

'Good morning...!' he whispered and dipped his head to nip at her lips; they were soft and sweet. He lifted his head and looked into her eyes and smiled once more before he again went down to kiss her, pulling her closer to him.

'Zain...'

'Shh...'

'Zain... I need to go back to *Daadijaan's* room... she will wake up soon...'

He closed his eyes and nuzzled his face into her neck, breathing in her fragrance, which was now mingled with his shower gel.

'Zain...' Sara had now started gently pushing his arms from around her...

'Zain... Please... I have to go... it will be very embarrassing.'

Zain sighed, cupped her face close, kissed her deeply and then rolled away...

Sara suddenly found herself free. Her lips were still tingling from his last kiss and she suddenly felt a chill as her cover had moved, but she quickly gathered herself and slipped out of the bed, lest he changed his mind.

Zain turned to watch her, resting his head against the pillows. Zorro had quietly come to lick her feet and was purring near her toes. She reached down and tickled him under his chin, looked at Zain and then turned around and quickly opened the garden door and shut it behind her.

Zain sighed and checked his watch. It was 5:15 in the morning... very early, but he felt quite rested. He buried his head into the pillow where her head had rested a few minutes ago and tried to go back to sleep.

Ten minutes later, he threw back the covers... sat up, got off the bed and opened the garden door once again. Zain almost headed towards *Daadijaan's* room to get her back... when Zorro let out a little bark, stopping Zain just in time... as it ran off chasing a squirrel.

Zain stopped... took a deep breath, turned around and went back to his room. He would go for a run. He needed to sort out his head...

Zain snapped out of his thoughts and found himself standing in front of his bed. He quickly made it and headed to change. *Daadijaan* and her picnic... god help them all!!

Zain joined the rest of the family at the front porch. There was general chaos all around, as usual everyone was talking at the same time, and Zorro was jumping around excited as well, adding to the commotion.

'Zorro! Here boy... quiet... quiet... down!' Zain bent down next to Zorro, calming him down.

'Everyone, calm down! What is happening? We will never leave if we continue like this...'

'We are wondering how many cars to take,' Saif spoke up.

'I was suggesting we take two cars and pile in...' he continued.

'No...let us take three cars in case one breaks down and then I can take the third car and drive Sara to see the Golden Gate bridge.' Zain spoke firmly.

'Yes, that makes sense...' agreed his father.

'Armaan, I will travel with you and Sara,' *Daadijaan* announced before anyone could say anything. 'Jahanaara will you go with Saif? He drives too fast for me...' glaring at a protesting Saif... 'also, if you reach earlier than us, you can organise the food there... Girls you go with your Zain *bhai*... *and* Zorro.'

'Oh, god... I am going to need ear plugs!!' Zain cursed.

'Don't worry Zain *bhai*... we won't bother you... We are carrying our own.' Both girls stuck their tongues out at Zain.

Zain watched *Daadijaan* take Sara's hand and lead her to his father's car. She wasn't even making an attempt to look at him. He got into his car and waited for the girls to pile in, when Zorro suddenly barked and sprinted out of the car, 'Zorro...where is he going...?'

'Zain *bhai*... he doesn't want to come with us... I think he prefers Sara's company to ours... ha ha...' responded Zoya.

Zain shook his head and clicked on the ignition and followed the other cars out. This place they were headed to was about some distance away. He looked forward to the drive. He didn't get much of a chance to drive in New York.

The picnic was a lot of fun. They reached well in time and the spot *Daadijaan* had chosen was scenically very beautiful and had a little stream flowing near it.

The weather had been perfect and they lazed around in the sun, played a few board games and the younger lot went for a little trek up the stream.

Sara enjoyed herself thoroughly, and also got a feel of how Zain and his brother and sisters must have grown up. It was a little different from her childhood, as they had been all girls, but the warmth they shared was very similar. All the siblings looked up to Zain as he was actually much older than them. Saif and the twins were closer to each other in age and were still quite casual with each other, but they were a little in awe of their older brother. It was very clear.

As they were wrapping up, *Daadijaan* who had been beaming the entire afternoon watching her family spend time together around her, chirped up, 'Zain you had better leave with Sara, if you want to catch the sunset. We will wrap up, head back and meet both of you at home.'

Sara turned towards *Daadijaan* to excuse herself and found Zain picking up his car keys,

'Let's go… we will need to leave now…'

Sara hugged *Daadijaan* and followed Zain to his car. She slid into the front seat next to him and waved at everyone as they left. Zain tuned in to a music channel playing some nice music while Sara looked out of her window trying to calm her nerves. This was the first time she was alone with Zain since this morning. She had felt his gaze on her a number of times during the picnic, their hands had touched as well occasionally, but other than that nothing else.

Zain had his shades on so was able to on and off glance in Sara's direction. He could see her side profile as she was looking out of her window. Before he turned on to the highway, Zain suddenly pulled over in a secluded shaded spot and before Sara realised what was happening, she felt herself being pulled towards him and felt her lips locked with his. Her initial reaction was to freeze, but it soon led to a thaw and the kiss turned very passionate, with both of them not wanting to let the other one go. Zain reached over to unclip her seatbelt, but Sara stopped him just in time.

'NO Zain! Not here please… Let's go… Please…' she pleaded.

Zain looked at her with a sharp expression on his face. He looked down at her lips…and then moved away…pushing back into his own seat, he ran his hand through his hair, flicked his shades back on, clicked the ignition on and turned the steering wheel back towards the highway.

Sara finally sighed and breathed a little easy, closing her eyes for a few minutes, she let the air conditioning cool her heated face. She reached down to the side pocket near her seat and took a sip of water to cool her throat. After a few minutes, she sat back again and looked ahead. Sara looked towards Zain and decided to start asking him questions to break the tension between them.

Zain figured out what she was doing, 'What is this? What is that? Oh! How beautiful… How far is this…?' She was asking a tirade of questions to distract him… and ease the tension. She knew very well what he wanted to do… Hell! What they both wanted…but, okay… he would play along…

He quietly answered all her questions in his deep voice… until they finally reached the viewing point for the Golden Gate bridge. The sun was just about to set and it was really beautiful. Zain loved this spot as well and had many memories of driving up there sometimes alone or sometimes with a girl he had been dating at that time. The sunset here never lets you down...

As they parked and got out of the car, Zain watched Sara come and stand in front and lean back against the hood... he could see she was in awe of what she saw in front of her. Everything looked golden and the setting sun against the sea with the Golden Gate silhouette was breathtaking.

Sara stood... watching... her lips parted, arms folded in front of her... her eyes wide taking it all in...

Zain stood a little to the side watching her. His view had the sunset, the sea, the bridge and Sara... all breathtaking. He almost reached out for her and kissed her when he realised there were many other cars around with youngsters making out like he used to when he was their age. He wouldn't want to embarrass Sara here. So he stood and watched her... while she watched the sunset...

After a while, it started to get dark as the sun had set. Sara looked towards Zain and followed him back into the car. Before they left the place, she turned to him and placed her hand gently on his arm as he moved to start the car, 'Thank you... this was really beautiful...'

Zain looked at her, his eyes following her lips as she spoke. He reached over and gently kissed her. The kiss didn't last too long as they were interrupted by the honking and hooting around them.

Zain shook his head, smiling to himself. Even after all these years, things hadn't changed.

Sara blushed and sat back, while Zain reached over and started the car, turning the steering wheel in the direction of home.

[19]

By the time they reached home, everyone was already at the dinner table and generally chatting. Zain and Sara had driven home in silence and had gotten out of the car without a word to each other and headed inside. They were pulled into the conversation about the next day's barbeque and family coming in to join them. Though the two of them were quieter than the rest, no one really noticed them and the general bonhomie continued.... Finally *Daadijaan* declared that she was tired and wanted to take her pills and sleep well as she was excited about the next day, which was actually her birthday. They had zoom calls planned with family in India and other relatives across the world...

As Daadijaan got up from the table, Sara also got up to escort her, when Daadijaan stopped her and told her to stay and spend time with the others. Zain got up instead and said he was still tired from his week of travel and would call it a night, so would escort Daadijaan. He didn't even look at the others and helped *Daadijaan* out.

His parents were the next to call it a day and Sara was left with Saif and the twins. The girls wanted to watch a film and hearing the name of the film, Saif begged to be excused. Sara politely joined the girls for a while and then half way through excused herself as well, saying she was tired and it had already gotten quite late.

She slipped into *Daadijaan's* room and could hear *Daadijaan's* rhythmic breathing. Her sleeping pills kicked in very quickly. Sara changed into her night clothes and slipped into bed next to the sleeping lady. She shut her eyes and all she could think of was Zain and her kissing. She opened her eyes and turned on her side, hoping to wipe her mind clean, clamping her eyes shut, she tried desperately to fall asleep. She did this for twenty minutes… with no success.

Then sitting up in bed, she made up her mind. Sliding out of the bed very quietly, she tiptoed to the garden exit and carefully opened it hoping to find Zain outside with Zorro. But, she found no one there. She quietly walked across the garden patch to Zain's room wondering how to enter as she saw no light on inside. She put her hand on the knob and tried to turn it, but it was shut.

Sara tried to calm her nerves… she could go back to *Daadijaan's* room… and regret it… or she could knock… She had to knock…!

Biting her lip she raised her knuckle to the glass pane of the door and knocked gently… twice. There was no answer. She knocked again… and waited. Again, there was no answer. Taking a deep breath, Sara sighed and turned around… and was about to take a step when she heard the door open and Zain was standing there.

'Sara?'

Before he could finish saying her name, she ran to him and hugged him. Holding her close, he looked down at her and found her reaching up to pull his head down to kiss him.

'What?'

When they finally broke apart to take a breath, Sara looked at Zain and said, 'Zain, I need you...!'

Zain immediately pulled her hand and took her into his room, shutting the door as soon as she entered. He pulled Sara gently to him, nuzzling her neck, 'Sara...tonight I cannot just sleep next to you...'

She kissed him and looked him in the eye, 'Neither can I... I need you Zain..'

Zain lifted her up and carried her to his bed, lying her down gently. He lay down beside her, framing her face in his hands while he kissed her and sucked on her lips. Slowly his hands moved down to cover her soft breasts gently rubbing against a nipple making it harden even through her T-shirt and thin bra. He was watching her while he did this. He didn't remember being this gentle with any of the women he had slept with earlier, but with Sara, he felt he needed to.

His hand moved lower grazing the little skin that had been exposed as her T-shirt had ridden up. He felt her stiffen as his fingertips touched her bare skin. Her eyes were closed, she was trying very hard to keep herself calm.

'Relax,' he whispered against her lips as his hands explored her navel inched lower. Sara latched on to his lips pulling him closer. He broke away and discarded his T-shirt. Sara watched him and realised that she had never seen him shirtless. In all the days she had slept next to him, she hadn't seen him bare chested and he hadn't seen her without her clothes either.

Suddenly both of them realised they couldn't wait any longer and frantically grabbed each other, discarding clothes which went flying in all directions. They couldn't keep their hands off each other. Zain held her close, fondling her breasts, sucking on her nipples and spreading her legs wide with his own, making space for himself, straining against her...trying to control himself.

Sara's hands were roaming up and down the rippling muscles of his back, she looked up at him as he moved over her, moving her hands to his chest and face... pulling him down closer... he stopped moving and looked at her... hoping she was okay, as he couldn't wait any longer.

Sara reached out and pulled him closer from his waist. That was all the encouragement he needed. Quickly moving away to don some protection, Zain moved back to hold her, sinking into her, slowly pushing against her. He gently nudged his way in... and realised he didn't face much resistance... She was so wet that after an initial barrier he slid right in. He was watching her face as he did this. Zain could see her clenching her lips as she felt a shooting pain, but soon calmed her breathing and adjusted herself to him and her hands moved to his lower back, pulling him closer.

Zain kissed her neck as he felt her resistance end and slowly started to move, all the while using his lips to nuzzle her breasts or her neck. Sara held him close as she moved with him, she had never felt like this. Her hands were laced with his over her head as he moved with force inside her. She felt herself moving into a spiral of sensation, the magical feeling increasing with Zain's every thrust and grind, she was losing control.

After a while, she realised she was lost! His final thrusts, till he suddenly stopped moving, took her over the edge. She called out his name as she climaxed and her mouth was covered by his. Each holding on to each other while their climax lasted.

After what seemed like a long time, both of them started to stir. Zain lifted his head from her shoulder and rolled off her, taking her with him. Tucking her into his side, he covered them both with his blanket. He held her close with his hand covering her soft breast and gently rubbing against her nipple. Slowly they could feel their breathing settle, and Zain whispered into her ear… 'Sleep!'

They felt something soft climb on to the bed and settle near their feet, looking down they found Zorro had made himself comfortable. Smiling at each other, Zain snuggled in and gradually drifted off to sleep.

'Zain… Zain!'

Zain stirred as he heard his name being called. He moved his head towards the source of the sound and kissed the lips as his name was whispered the third time. His eyes were still shut, but he knew he was smiling as he kissed her and then nuzzled her neck. He held her even closer with one arm, moving his other hand down over her body.

'Zain… Listen… I need to go to *Daadijaan's* room…'

'Why?' He growled as he kissed her ear.

'What do you mean, why?' Sara giggled, 'How can I stay here…?'

'What time is it?' Zain sighed and opened his eyes

'I think it is 4 am… *Daadijaan* wakes up in a while to say her prayers… last time I just about made it…'

'Shhhh...' Zain stopped her mid sentence, kissing her gently. His hands moved up to cover her breast, flicking and cupping them, reaching down and following his hands with his lips and tongue. Sara shivered with every touch.

Her hands were in his hair pulling him closer. She could feel him growing against her thigh and right on cue, Zain lifted himself to settle himself in between her legs. He looked up at her, and started to slide lower, kissing her body as he moved, stopping to dip his tongue into her belly button, his hands still on her breasts. He looked up at her and into her eyes as she raised her head to look at him, before he sank his mouth into her, his tongue licking and sucking her driving her over the edge.

She had never felt this way before. Sara desperately tried to grope for his head, trying to control what she was experiencing, stifling her cries of pleasure with her hand stuffed in her mouth. When she had started feeling herself calming down and coming back to reality, she saw Zain move up and kiss her on her lips and cheeks.

He looked into her eyes and whispered, 'Are you okay?'

Sara nodded and moved her hands to his face. She reached up and kissed him hungrily, matching his force with her own. She felt Zain adjust himself and move into her in one fluid motion. He nestled inside her feeling himself surrounded with her wet warmth. Licking her collarbone, he started to move gently and then quickly increased his rhythm. They were moving with urgency and passion, their breaths short and hurried, Sara again felt herself going into a spiral, she couldn't imagine herself feeling like this so quickly again. She looked at Zain's face as he brought his face level with hers, his eyes opening and closing as moved in and out of her. She spread her legs wider, giving him more space and bringing him closer at the same time.

Suddenly, Zain rolled her over, still inside her, bringing her to sit astride him. She looked down at him looking into her eyes. His hands moved up her waist to the sides of her breasts, fondling them, pinching her nipples as his fingers moved across them. He reached up and tucked her hair behind her ears, clearing his view of her as she sat on top of him.

'So beautiful...' he whispered, holding her hand and bringing her fingers to his lips.

He then moved up to holding her close half sitting up, he nuzzled and suckled her, bringing her down to lean over him. Her hair framed her face, she bit her lips as she felt him against her breast. His hands slowly moved down to her waist, guiding her to start moving, she started to ride him slowly, moving up and down, sometimes grinding against him. His hand holding her by her waist and her own hands sprayed on his chest as she kept her balance.

Both of them quickly reached their spiralling phase, quickening their pace as she rode him with urgency. Sara realised she couldn't hold on any longer when at that same point she felt him also clenching her by the waist and as he felt her climax, he moved her off him and brought her to lie down next to him holding her close. Only then did he permit his own release, and she felt him shudder next to her thigh as he held her tightly and brought his lips down on hers, his kiss, first forceful and then turning gentle as his climax subsided.

It took Sara some time to come out of her blissful state. She realised Zain had been careful as this time he hadn't had time to wear any protection. After a few minutes, she tugged at Zain's arm which was draped across her, whispering, 'I need to go, Zain.'

Zain reluctantly let her go...Sara slid off the bed and put on her clothes. Suddenly very shy and thankful that the room was dark. Embarrassed as she remembered herself sitting in that wanton state astride Zain. She felt her face heat up and turn red as she slipped on her top. Zorro stirred and nuzzled her as she moved around, glancing on and off at Zain who was watching her move around.

She saw him also get out of the bed and reach for his clothes. Pulling on a sweatshirt over his T-shirt, Zain walked towards her. Reaching down, he tipped her face up and kissed her lips gently, his tongue finding hers, his arms holding her close.

'Zain...' Sara gently put her hands against his chest, 'This isn't helping..'

Zain checked the time. It was almost time for *Daadijaan* to wake up for her prayers. He looked at Sara.

'Go grab something warm and meet me outside near the gate. We can take Zorro for a walk.'

Sara nodded and slipped out of the room. Once in the other room, she quickly used the washroom, freshened up, looking at her face in the mirror in front of her, she realised she felt shy at just looking at herself. What had just happened? She had willingly let it happen, so decided to go with the flow. After a few minutes, grabbing her red sweatshirt and scarf, Sara was just about to leave the room when *Daadijaan* stirred.

'Where are you going, *Beta*... so early.'

'Just thought I would take Zorro for a walk. I think Zain let him out, I will see you in a bit of *Daadijaan.*' Sara replied softly.

'Okay, but don't tire yourself out... we have a full day today as well.'

Sara suddenly remembered.

'Oh, Happy Birthday *Daadijaan*! I brought something for you, and will give it to you at breakfast...'

'You didn't have to... sweetheart... now run along otherwise we will have a sulking Zain...'

Sara froze. 'a sulking Zain...' did that mean *Daadijaan* had guessed?

She shyly looked at *Daadijaan* and saw the old lady giving her a knowing smile...Embarrassed, Sara smiled and slipped out of the room.

She hurried down the corridor and almost bumped into Zain.

'What took you so long? I thought *Daadijaan* had asked you to join her in her prayers as well... Let's go... Zorro is getting restless...'

They walked down the hill silently, with Zorro trotting in front...scampering up ahead and then coming back to them. As they reached an opening in the thicket, Zorro scampered on to a path between the trees. Zain nodded at Sara nudging her to follow Zorro. The path seemed to be a well-worn one and familiar to both Zain and Zorro. They walked for a few minutes in silence listening to the sounds of birdsong and also enjoying the soft early morning sunshine. Zain pointed out things familiar to him, reaching out to steady her every now and then.

The path opened up towards the edge of a cliff and they suddenly got a clear view of the Bay and San Francisco city beyond it. The view was stunning! The sky was clear with a few feathery clouds dotting it. The sun was slowly inching its way upwards, the water glistening... the city glittering in the background, an array of colours... and shiny bits where the sun was reflecting off the glass buildings. Sara loved what she saw, it was like a painting! Sara stopped walking and just stood there to watch and take in the beauty.

Zain came up and stood next to her. He took her hand in his and laced his fingers through hers.

'Wah *bhai*! If someone could take a photograph it would look like those happily ever after photographs we see in stock photos.'

Both Zain and Sara jumped, hearing Saif's voice just behind them.

Zain pushed her hand away making Sara gasp.

'What are you doing here Saif?' Zain asked casually, though clearly sounding annoyed.

'Out for a walk, but what is more interesting is what the 'two of you' are doing here?'

Saif looked at his older brother with a knowing smile on his face, raising his eyebrow at Sara as well, who suddenly felt very foolish.

'We weren't doing anything! Just taking Zorro out for a run,' snapped Zain. Calling Zorro to him, he turned to his brother and Sara, 'It is time we went back...'

Sara looked inquiringly at Zain as they walked back towards the house, Saif carrying on a cheerful chatter with monosyllabic answers from them. As soon as they reached home, Zain headed straight to his room without even a glance at Sara.

Saif walked Sara to *Daadijaan's* room and winked at her. She blushed, but said nothing.

The rest of the day had gone, spending it with the family, Zoom calls with relatives all over the world. Sara even saw her sister, Saniya and brother-in-law Ashar, on the screen wishing *Daadijaan* and showing off her little nephew who was gurgling in Ashar's arms.

Lots of flowers arrived for *Daadijaan* through the day, even Sara's parents had sent an arrangement. She had told them about joining the family in San Francisco and her father had said they would also wish the grand old lady on that day.

Zain was busy with calls the entire morning and part of the afternoon. Joining the family only for a quick lunch. He had messaged her saying he would see her at lunch as he was stuck in some emergency meeting during the morning. She had responded with a single word, 'Okay!'

At lunch, he sat opposite her at the table and joined in on the banter and discussion about the menu for the evening. She had felt his eyes on her on and off, but had kept herself occupied chatting with the twins and *Daadijaan*. He excused himself after lunch and went back to shut himself away for a few hours of work. The twins dragged Sara with them to the salon in the afternoon and they had returned just in time to get ready before the other guests arrived.

'*Daadijaan*...I brought something small for you...' whispered Sara as she sat down next to the grand old lady, who was behaving as though she was the queen and was presiding over a royal court. All her invitees had arrived, the house looked grand with fairy lights everywhere. Each person had dressed in traditional clothes as she had requested and there was free flowing wine and food.

Daadijaan smiled and hugged her, opening the box that Sara was holding out for her. Inside it was a pendant with the map of Lahore in it. *Daadijaan* loved to talk about her childhood in Lahore.

'Thank you *meri jaan*! You didn't need to. Zain has already given me a lovely diamond bracelet. I am sure it is from both of you. This is beautiful too and something I shall treasure. Only you would think of something like this.'

Zain was standing at the bar listening to uncle Anwar talk about the stock market, he was also watching Sara. She was looking lovely in a light pink silk kurta and figure-hugging tights and a light gauzy scarf with delicate pearl earrings and some slim gold bangles on her wrists. She had done her face in her usual style, kohl lined eyes and just some naked gloss on her lips, but for some reason her cheeks were looking a little more rosy than normal. She was in fact glowing.

Zain watched Sara sit down next to *Daadijaan* and hand her a box. He saw her blush at something and then heard *Daadijaan* call out to his mother.

'Jahaanara, come and see what Sara has brought for me. Armaan *dekho*... a pendant with the map of Lahore... my first love.'

Both Zain's parents smiled at her and Jahaanara even kissed her on her forehead. This made Zain uncomfortable.

Daadijaan could be heard telling one of their relatives how she was so touched with Sara's gift and that she hadn't needed to do this as Zain had already given her a present which she was sure was from both of them. Zain stiffened.

He could hear the relative ask, 'Both of them? How come? What was the connection...?'

No one actually knew Sara at the gathering other than the immediate family. No one in the US or extended family had ever been told about the *nikaah* and the drama in India four years ago.

So, no one had introduced her. Everyone quietened down listening to what *Daadijaan* had to say.

'Oh, *ho*! How silly of us, We never introduced Sara. Everyone, Sara is Zain's wife!'

Sara also turned towards Daadijan in shock. She hadn't ever been called that in public.

There was silence. Sara's eyes quickly searched for Zain, hoping to find him. She found him frozen to a spot and his face very grim.

'Aare, we never told anyone, but I got them married four years ago. It was such a drama! You all will never believe how my headstrong grandson had to marry Sara much against his wishes, but as per my wishes!! After all, I am Zubeida Begum and no one goes against my wishes. And, in the end I know my decision is the right one...' *Daadijaan* gloated, she loved playing the drama queen.

Zain muttered under his breath, dug his hands into his trouser pocket and quietly walked out of the party. Both Armaan and Jahaanara anxiously looked at each other. They knew their son, he hated being told or forced to do anything and that once that he had given in had been terrible for him.

All around though there seemed to be a lot of excitement. Everyone was talking at the same time. A lot of people were coming up to her to meet her. Zain's parents and *Daadijaan* were also surrounded with relatives and friends congratulating them.

Sara was still in shock. She tried to smile at everyone who came up to speak to her. She couldn't create more drama now and spoil *Daadijaan's* party. Fielding a hundred questions that were being thrown at her, Sara kept trying to see if she could find Zain.

How could he leave her here alone in this situation?

Sara had been sitting next to *Daadijaan* for the past hour meeting people. 'She's Zain's wife!' still rung in her ears. Looking around, she saw everyone busy - some talking and having animated discussions, some laughing, in one corner she could see Saif and the twins lounging around with their other friends and cousins. For some reason she couldn't see Zain and what was more intriguing was that no one was actually asking for him after the initial excitement. Sara suddenly felt tired. She couldn't wait for the evening to end and wanted to go back home with Zain. Then she stopped herself, New York was not home. It was Zain's home.

She waited patiently with the family till everyone left and then walked with *Daadijaan* to their room. The old lady was still beaming. She had loved her party and was thrilled with how everything had turned out.

Walking down the corridor, she held Sara's hand and said, 'You know Sara, I am so happy I was able to tell everyone about you and Zain...'

Sara suddenly spotted Zain coming out of his room. He froze when he heard what Daadijan said.

Daadijaan was still talking, 'It has been over four years and it is now about time Zain realises I was right with what I did.'

Sara saw Zain scowl and clench his fists. He looked through her, glaring at his grandmother, who was oblivious to his presence. Zain turned around and went back to his room and slammed the door shut.

[20]

Sara waited for *Daadijaan* to fall asleep, changed into her night clothes and slipped out of the room and walked quietly towards Zain's. She needed to speak to him, she needed to have him hold her... she needed to just see him. Reaching the door, she wrapped her fingers around the knob expecting it to quietly give way and open, but it didn't. She tugged at it, twisting it to both sides, but it didn't open. Had he forgotten to leave it unlocked? He must have.

She gently knocked on the door twice and waited.

There was no response...

'Zain?' Sara knocked once again and called out his name. Still no response. Why was he not letting her in? Was he not there?

Sara waited outside for another five minutes and then started feeling a little cold. Wrapping her hands around herself, she slowly walked back to *Daadijaan's* room, quite puzzled.

A little while before Sara went to Zain's room, Armaan and Jahaanara were nervously looking at their eldest son. He was standing in front of them with a look on his face which they had anticipated. Eyebrows knitted together, a very grim and serious expression on his face, eyes flashing anger and they knew his fists were clenched even though they couldn't see them as he had his arms folded across his chest. Zain was otherwise obedient and well brought up, but even as a child he had hated being forced to do anything. He never gave them any reason to force him to do anything, but they knew of his attitude towards this one thing.

Both Zain's parents had been surprised when they saw Zain with Sara, they seemed to be getting along, they liked Sara and had just the night before discussed the fact that they thought there might be no need for an annulment and that Sara and Zain might just make a great couple... and then this...

Zain had been patient with his grandmother, almost forgiving her for what she had done. His having Sara staying with him had made him soften towards her as well. However, *Daadijaan's* gloating about her role in the entire episode in India had struck Zain's ego again, and he had never really forgiven his grandmother. His parents were a little nervous about what he intended to do.

Zain was standing in front of his parents. 'I am heading to the airport...'

'Now? At this time of the night?'

'Yes, I need to get to London as soon as possible.'

'But you were going to go back to New York with Sara tomorrow...' stammered his mother, a little nervously.

'No, I am not now...'

'What about Sara?'

'She can travel without me... the same way she came here... she isn't a child.'

Zain's parents exchanged glances.

'Zain, we know you are angry with what your grandmother has been saying... but...' Jahaanara tried to reason with her son.

'But nothing Mum...there is nothing. Sara isn't my wife... she wasn't then either... I hate it when decisions are made about my life without my being involved in it... and you know that...' Zain exploded.

'Yes we do, but you know your grandmother...' his father tried to get a word in.

'Yes, I know my grandmother and I know how manipulating she can be... I have had enough...'

'But, we thought... you and Sara...' his mother whispered anxiously.

'What about me and Sara...? Do you also think we should be together, just because *Daadijaan* forced us into a *Nikaah* over four years ago...' He looked at them accusingly.

'Well I don't...There is nothing between us, I will not let *Daadijaan* get her way this time. I have had enough.' Zain threw his hands up and headed towards the door.

'But Zain...'

'I am leaving, *Baba*, I will call you from London...' he turned to speak to his father.

'Sara finishes her assignment in New York in a few weeks. She can go back to India then as her parents had told us she would. We can send the annulment papers in the next few months.' He turned towards the door.

'Zain, have you spoken to Sara about this?' his mother asked him quietly.

'NO!... And, there is no need...'

'Zain...!' his father called out, his voice going a pitch higher than before.

'*Baba*... I am done. I will leave the car at the airport, please have it collected.'

'Will call you once I land in London.' saying this, Zain turned around, picked up his suitcase which he had left outside their door and headed out without even looking back. He was seething.

[21]

Sara had a restless night and spent most of the time pacing the room and then tossed and turned the rest. Finally, she told herself, I will speak to him tomorrow, anyway since they were on the same flight back to New York, they would have enough time.

Sara smiled at the family as she joined them at the breakfast table. They would need to leave in an hour to catch their flight. She looked around, but couldn't see Zain anywhere. Zorro came and settled by her feet, and she smiled and tickled him under his jaw. As Sara sat down, she realised there was a lull in the conversation at the table.

'Armaan uncle, I am all packed. *Daadijaan* I hope you enjoyed your party, 80 is a special number. Jahaanara aunty, thank you for inviting me as well. I had a wonderful time.' Sara tried to cover up her anxiety.

'No, No, *beta*, we are very happy you joined us, it was lovely to meet you. *Daadijaan* specially asked for you to be here. You are practically family...' Jahaanara smiled at Sara.

'She is Zain's wife... not practically family... Jahaanara! Say it the way it is... I did nothing wrong by announcing it last night. It is the truth! Now if that son of yours wants to misbehave, dismiss it and run away from the truth just to feed his ego, then I have nothing more to say!' *Daadijaan* spoke with a loud and stern voice.

Sara stared at *Daadijaan*. Her eyes wide. She looked from one person to the other.

'Uncle...Zain?' Sara stuttered anxiously, quite confused with what was being spoken about.

'*Ammi*!!! Please!!' Zain's mother threw up her hands in exasperation. She couldn't believe her mother-in-law was still sticking to her own drama.

'*Beta...*' he hesitated, 'he had to leave last night!' Zain's father tried to calm things down and replied to Sara's unfinished question...

'Zain was suddenly called to the London office, so left last night itself. Don't you worry, Saif will drop you to the airport.' He turned to Saif and nodded. 'Zain said you have your swipe card to the apartment so you should go back to New York. I am sure he will call you and speak to you later.'

Sara was stunned. Zain had left... without even speaking to her.

She glanced down at her phone, no message either!

'Sara,' Saif spoke up, 'Why don't you finish eating, the girls and I will drop you to the airport. We have to anyway bring Zain's car back from there, okay?'

Sara quickly finished eating and went to collect her things. She found Zain's grandmother sitting in the room counting her beads.

Swallowing slowly, Sara walked up to the old lady and reached out and hugged her. 'Khuda hafiz, *Daadijaan*! I am leaving now. I will call and speak with you after I reach and hopefully will see you soon.'

The old lady didn't say anything, she had tears in her eyes and hugged her back, silently blessing her.

It was fairly late by the time Sara let herself into Zain's apartment. She had to keep stopping herself when she referred to it as home. The flight back had been long and she had kept checking her phone to see if Zain had left her any message, but he hadn't. She controlled herself and didn't message or call either. She would do it after she reached it.

Rolling her suitcase into the study, Sara fixed herself a mug of *chai* and checked her phone once again. Still no call or message.

Sara bit her lower lip, gripping her mug, she stepped outside into the deck. Setting her mug down, she finally sighed deeply and picked her phone up. Clicking on Zain's name, she called him. The phone rang and rang, but he didn't pick up...

Sara, picked up her mug and phone and went back inside. She changed and walked up to Zain's room and got into his bed. Picking up her phone, she called his number again. But it kept ringing.

Putting her phone away, she slid under the covers and tried to sleep, but couldn't. Her mind was racing in circles. What had happened? What was it that *Daadijaan* had said at the table? Why had Zain left? Everything had been fine till just before the party, not just fine, but it had been excellent.

Sara lay looking up at the ceiling. She was very confused. Had she done or said something ?

She sat up and reached for her phone again. It must be 6 am in London, he would be awake, that is, if he ever slept at all! The past few weeks had proved that neither of them was getting any sleep without each other.

Sara typed in three question marks and sent it to Zain. She could see he had read it immediately as she saw the blue ticks flash, so she waited for him to respond. But, he didn't.

She could feel tears well up in her eyes slowly. It took a while, but Sara then cried herself to sleep.

Zain had taken the earliest flight out of San Francisco to London. His London office wasn't expecting him so he knew they would be surprised. Sending his manager a message, Zain saw his phone buzz. Saif had sent him some photographs from the party... the party he had walked out of.

Zain swiped through the photographs grimacing. Saif had sent him only photographs that had Sara in it. Clenching his fists, Zain deleted each one, one by one... till he reached the last one. It was a solo shot of her licking her lips... with her eyes looking out, as though she was looking for someone or something.

Sighing deeply, he sent the last picture to his trash can.

He had made up his mind. It had to end. He had to prove his grandmother wrong.

Zain reached London and drove straight to the office. He had lined up a bag full of meetings for the next few days. He would try and see if he could also manage a few more days in Paris. In between meetings, checking messages on his phone, he found himself clicking on his trash can and on the photograph of Sara that he had sent there. He clicked on retrieve and saved it, telling himself he would delete it for good later.

Shutting his eyes for a few seconds and clenching and unclenching his fists, trying to focus on his work at the office, Zain went into his next meeting.

He spoke to his father later in the day, so was aware that Sara had gone back to New York. He also got a message from his brother saying, '*Bhai*, call her!'

Ignoring everything, he went without calling or messaging her. He had decided and he would stick with his decision.

Zain had heard his phone ring and had seen her name flash a few times. He was sitting in his hotel room nursing a drink cursing loudly, he threw his phone on the bed and went to take a shower. He hadn't been able to sleep the entire night.

As he walked back into the room, he heard his phone buzz and saw her message. Checking his watch, he realised it must have been 2-3 am in the morning and she hadn't been able to sleep... like him.

Gritting his teeth together, he told himself... they would both get used to it.

Sara spent the next few days buried in the library and museum, she was at the end of her project and assignment and needed to defend her submission. She needed to do it well and the current problem or confusion in her life was only distracting her. Sara had spoken to her father the night before and her ticket for the end of the month was booked. She would leave the day after her project defence.

Zain's parents and Saif had called every day to check on her, as had *Daadijaan*, but she didn't have much to tell them. She was able to speak to Saif a little more as he asked her more pointed questions unlike the others who asked her how she was etc.,

He asked, 'Has *bhai* called?' 'Have you called him?' 'Did he tell you when he was coming back?' and she answered as honestly as she could.

She wasn't able to sleep too well and most nights did go to sleep only because she was exhausted.

She hadn't had any news from Zain. He hadn't called, not even messaged...

[22]

Sara entered Zain's apartment and stood there at the door for some time. It had been a week since she had returned from San Francisco.

It was early evening, she wasn't hungry. Sara made her way to Zain's bar, found a bottle of wine and took a goblet. Pouring herself some of the burgundy liquid, she made her way to the deck. Sitting down on one of the chairs, Sara tucked her feet under her and pulled the wrap kept there to cover her shoulders. Looking out into the dark expanse in front of her with the glittering lights on either side, had a calming feeling on her.

Zain, walked into the apartment building dragging his suitcase behind him.

Max smiled at him and fist pumped like he always did.

'Perfect timing Mr Zain. Sara got in half an hour ago.'

Zain forced a smile on his face and walked ahead. Changing it back to the scowl he had arrived with, he thought to himself, 'Okay… this needed to be sorted out!'

He entered the apartment and glanced around. Noticing the doors to the deck open, he looked around his living room for any other clues. He found a bottle of wine on the counter. Running his hands through his hair, he walked over to the bar, fixed himself a stiff drink, picked up her bottle of wine and walked out to the deck. Topping up her glass, he sat down with his drink, without even glancing at her direction.

Sara was a little startled when she heard someone behind her. Zain…she looked up at him and watched him top up her drink and sit down next to her on the other chair swirling his own drink around in the glass.

'How was London?' She asked quietly, breaking the silence.

A growl was all she got in response. They continued to look out in front of them in silence.

Zain then suddenly drew his breath in sharply, leant forward, resting his elbows on his knees. Without looking towards her, he spat out, 'For how long has this plan been going on?'

Sara jumped. It took her a few seconds to process what he was saying.

'Plan? What plan?'

'This plan with *Daadijaan*… in retrospect now it all looks so beautifully planned and executed!' Zain growled.

Sara, totally confused and unsure, whispered, 'What are you talking about?'

'The entire thing that happened four years ago was *Daadijaan's* doing. I was forced into it and hated being manipulated.' Zain spoke, a harsh tone in his voice very evident.

'And, you think I was in this game with *Daadijaan*…?' Sara was trying to fathom what he was getting at.

'All those years ago, you think I was in on it with her... really Zain?'

'Or did you think that I came to New York just to seduce you, and that was the plan I hatched with *Daadijaan*...' Sara couldn't believe it! She quickly got up from the chair clenching her fists.

She stomped out towards the door to go back in. Zain caught her hand as she passed. Sara caught her breath...even though she was totally pissed, one touch was all it took to make her head spin!

Zain's face was at the level of the hand. He had caught it to stop her. He saw her clenched fist immediately release as soon as he touched her. Shutting his own eyes, trying to keep his focus, he spat out, 'Not then... But now...!'

Sara looked down at him, 'You think... I went to San Francisco as a part of some plan? To do what, Zain?'

'Sara, we both heard *Daadijaan* make the announcement last week. She didn't even ask us. I saw your reaction to her announcement. You seemed to expect it. Was it what you all had planned? Make it public in front of everyone, so again I would have no choice!'

He had abruptly left her hand and walked away, but was now facing her as he spoke... looking straight at her accusingly.

'Do you really think she brought me here as a part of some plan?' Sara still couldn't get what he was saying.

'Yes, a plan to make me comply, something I had vowed I wouldn't do.' Zain snapped.

Zain turned to look out into the sky, 'I knew something was up when she made *Baba* not send the annulment immediately, but I gave her a second chance. No one can do this to their own children, but she has and it wouldn't be possible if you hadn't helped her.'

Shaking his head, he turned to her, 'I cannot believe it... how could I have been such a fool?'

'Zain... Why would I do this?' Sara asked him with disbelief in her eyes. 'If you remember I was 18 and a child when all this happened and I had no idea what the hell was going on...I wasn't asked either...just to remind you...'

'You have been in touch with *Daadijaan* all these years. It is all so clear. You helped her complete her game. It was so easy, wasn't it?'

Sara's eyes were flashing and she could feel her head about to split.

'So you mean to say, you think the past five months of us being here together,' 'Us'... she couldn't get herself to say, 'was all something I planned with *Daadijaan*? And, it didn't mean anything to you at all?'

'I don't care if it did... it doesn't anymore!' Zain almost shouted.

'Now, that I know what is happening and I have control, there is no way this is going to be successful.' He clenched his fists into tight balls as he spoke.

'It is best if we go our own ways. You have two weeks left here. I won't throw you out, though by God, I want to! I will leave for London tomorrow and will stay out. Finish up whatever you need to and leave.' Zain picked up his glass and stomped into the apartment. Slamming his glass down on the counter, he walked up to his room as quickly as he could, shutting the door behind him as if it helped him shut the entire chapter from his life.

Sara was still in shock with what she had heard. Trembling and trying hard to control her tears, she picked up her own glass, walked into the kitchen and rinsed hers and Zain's discarded glass. She could feel tears rolling down her face. Entering the study, she shut the door as well.

[23]

Zain worked through the night to keep his mind off what had just happened. Work was what helped him last time and it would do the same now as well.

He had booked himself on an early morning flight to London and would be gone before she woke up. He would be gone for two days and then needed to plan to avoid her while she was still in the city.

Sara woke up from a night of restlessness and fitful sleep. It took her a few minutes to recall everything that had taken place the previous night.

She still could not believe that Zain thought her coming to New York and 'seducing' him was all a part of the plan. She got out of bed, and as she showered, she also realised that there was no point in her even trying to make him see reason. For him it was over and she was the villain!

'Okay!' she told herself, 'Let us get the next few weeks over.' She needed to take each day at a time as the next few weeks were crucial for her work. She had to focus.

Sara buried herself in work for the next two days, leaving early and coming back very late.

On Thursday, she had been convinced by her colleagues to join them for lunch outside in a café they frequented. It was Alice's birthday and it was nice to have a diversion. Sara enjoyed their company. They were bright, intelligent and fun and she liked Alice in particular, they had become good friends over the past few months. Sitting outside in the sun, chatting with them had helped cheer her up a bit, when Alice, who was sitting next to her, jumped up from her chair and went to hug someone who was passing by. Everyone turned to see who it was.

'Leyla... hey... it has been a while...' Alice said, hugging Leyla.

'Yes... it has. I spied you from across the courtyard and remembered it was your birthday... wanted to wish you...' Leyla smiled and hugged her friend...

'Guys...' said Alice, turning to her work friends who were watching the exchange, 'say hi to Leyla! Leyla and I have known each other since kindergarten.'

Leyla interrupted her, 'You were in Kindergarten darling, not me.'

Alice laughed at Leyla's words... 'and oh yes... Zain... her looooooong time friend.' she continued...

No one noticed, but Sara had stiffened a little while ago when she had seen Alice with Leyla. Her eyes had spotted Zain standing behind her as well, his eyes piercing hers.

She broke out of her trance at seeing Zain when she heard Alice introducing her friends to their group. 'Looong time friend...' those words stunned her. She had lived in the same house with Zain and he had never mentioned her... damn... how naïve had she been. Leyla must have been the girl Zain had brought home those many months ago after she had moved in.

'... and this is Sara...' She heard Alice's voice, 'we all work together at the MET.'

Leyla looked at Sara and then turned to Zain, 'Sara... are you from India?'

Gathering her wits together, Sara smiled and nodded.

'Zain isn't she... is she?' Leyla swivelled her pretty head between Sara's direction and Zain's.

'Sara, aren't you living in Zain's house? His relative from India who is here for a project or internship or something...?' Leyla asked aloud.

Sara slowly nodded, also aware that her colleagues were still watching this as an audience.

Zain continued to look at her with a steely glare only moving his arm around Leyla's waist.

Leyla laughed and snuggled into Zain, 'It is such a small world, Alice! How would I have known that your friend, Sara, is the same Sara who was staying at Zain's place and was also the reason why I haven't been able to go over as often as I did earlier...'

Sara gulped, licking her lips, aware that Zain was watching her blurted out, 'Please do not let me restrict you. Feel free to visit. It is, after all, not my house... it is Zain's,' She said his name out a little too loudly, 'and I usually stay most of the day at the museum and of late am spending most of my nights buried in work in my room. So please do not let me stop you.' Sara continued.

There was silence all around as everyone listened to Sara's monologue in response to Leyla's teasing remark.

Zain finally spoke in his trademark deep baritone, 'Sara, good to see you. Alice, happy birthday once again! Leyla, let's leave them to celebrate and not cramp their style. We have a reservation upstairs.' He pointed towards one of the most expensive restaurants across the street.

They smiled at everyone and made their way across the street. Sara busied herself scraping her fork across her plate and quickly drank up her water.

'Everyone, listen I have to run. I need to send off a few emails. You all forget I am on a very short time line and need to have everything submitted by the end of this month if I want to be able to catch my flight back home.'

The others nodded, but she knew they had many questions they wanted to ask, but were too polite to.

An hour later, while Sara was still deep into the manuscript she was studying, she realised someone had come and stood beside her workstation. Looking up, she realised it was Alice who was observing her quietly. Sara looked up and smiled at her.

'Need to chat?' Alice asked quietly.

Sara looked up at her friend, reached for her hand and shook her head, 'Thank you, am good.'

Sara could feel Alice hover around for a little while longer and then move away to her station. Sara loved this about her friends here, they weren't very intrusive, unlike her friends and family back home where everything everywhere was everyone's business. Sighing deeply, Sara went back to working on her manuscript. She needed to list all her references and double check them.

Zain was back at his office. He hadn't anticipated seeing Sara that afternoon. She looked happy with her friends. They seemed a jovial bunch. He had met Alice a few times with Leyla, but had never associated her with the museum. Sara didn't seem to be too affected by the events that had happened. Zain shook his head, why should she be? She was party to the entire thing. What Zain couldn't figure out was why she had agreed to it. What would she get out of it? Her family wasn't poor and he was sure they weren't in need of money. What could it have been? They had been okay with being not in touch and looking for an annulment... then why now?

Zain and Leyla had a pleasant lunch, with Leyla doing most of the talking. He noticed her nibbling on her food, ensuring that her fork didn't touch her perfectly made-up mouth, constantly checking to see her reflection in her spoon. She did mention how she was surprised to hear from him after many months. His excuse of being busy with work worked with her. It was always easy to sort things out with her.

Zain needed Leyla as a distraction. He quickly clicked her number again and fixed up dinner and drinks with their other friends. This would keep him out of the house as well. He might even spend the night with her. He needed it to get Sara out of his system.

Sara heard Zain come home in the evening. He went up to his room and she continued to work in one corner of the living room on her laptop. At around 7, the doorbell buzzed. Sara was about to get up to see who it was, when she saw Zain come down the stairs. Max must have pinged him to let him know who it was.

'Leyla...? I thought we were to meet at the club, I was just about to get ready.' She heard Zain's deep voice from the door.

'Zain... Yes, but I had gone shopping and bought a new dress. I then decided I would wear it tonight. So, instead of going all the way home to change, I thought it would be more sensible to change here.' Leyla replied as she walked into the living area, carrying many bags. She was still dressed in the clothes she was in at lunch.

She spotted Sara working in the corner and walked across the room. 'Hey!! Busy with work...?'

Sara started to smile and nod and then stiffened when she saw Zain standing behind her.

'Sad, you could have joined us if you were free, you would have fun.' Leyla went on, oblivious to the tension in the room.

'Zain, I am going up stairs to change, I think some of my stuff may still be here, I could use those...' Leyla's voice trailed off as she climbed the stairs to Zain's room.

Zain was still leaning against the breakfast counter looking at his phone. Sara tried not to glance at him and kept typing on her laptop, trying to look busy.

'Zain! Zain!' Leyla's voice could be heard from upstairs, 'Aren't you coming up to change? We need to be at the club in an hour...'

Sara looked up and could see Zain watching her. He straightened up and put his phone into his pocket and headed upstairs.

Sara closed her eyes. She couldn't imagine Zain and Leyla up in his room together. Her head was throbbing. She looked at her screen and realised she had typed a paragraph of total gibberish. Cursing herself, she shut her computer!

Sara walked to the kitchen and decided to make herself some chai. She needed something comforting.

Zain and Leyla were walking down the stairs, on their way out. He could smell the fragrance of the delicious *chai* she made. Leyla, herself, stopped and exclaimed, 'Yyummm! Sara smells so good. It reminds me of the *chai* in my grandparents' home in Agra. I wish we could stop and have some, but we are late!'

Sara looked at the two of them, 'Leyla your dress is very nice...!'

'Isn't it...? I loved it at the store and just had to have it. We should go shopping sometime soon...'

'Don't wait up... I will stay over at Leyla's tonight.' Zain's brusque voice made her look up at him.

'Ooh Zain!! I like the plan...' Leyla turned to him, draping herself over him.

Sara gulped and forced herself to smile back at them, 'Good night! Have fun!'

She was looking straight at Zain's dark eyes. He clenched his fists and then moved them up to steer Leyla towards the door.

As the door shut behind them, Sara drained her entire cup of tea in the sink and walked out onto the deck. She sat down in one corner and hugged her knees. What was happening? How did things become like this? How could he do this to her?

She still couldn't believe he thought she was doing this with his grandmother. Did what they shared mean nothing to him? As she closed her eyes and tried to calm her breath in between her sobs, she could see herself and Zain together in San Francisco. Did none of that mean anything to him?

Watching Zain with Leyla was killing her. He was going to spend the night with her tonight. Sara hugged her knees and wept. It suddenly dawned upon her, something she had known deep inside her, despite everything and how he had been behaving, she had fallen for him, and fallen bad. She suddenly wanted her mother. She very rarely felt like this...

[24]

Zain sat up in bed. It wasn't his bed, it was Leyla's. He turned to see her on the other side. They had gotten back pretty late and had started to make out. But, he just wasn't able to go through with it. Apologising to Leyla, blaming fatigue and too much alcohol, they had both agreed to sleep it off.

But Zain hadn't been able to sleep. Whenever he saw a bed, he saw Sara. He just couldn't do anything about it. He had tried.

Glancing at his watch he saw it was 4 am, they had gotten to Leyla's only an hour ago and now she had passed out. Getting out of Leyla's bed, Zain gathered his things. Picking up his jacket, he headed for the front door. He was going to go home. Sara would definitely be asleep by now.

Sara woke up to a wet pillow and her sheets tangled around her legs, she had hardly been able to sleep and had tossed and turned the entire night, finally passing out only around 4 am, just before Zain had come back. She was oblivious to the fact that Zain had come home and sat watching her for almost half an hour silently, watching her toss and turn, almost picking her up and taking her upstairs to his room. It had been very tough on him to not do that. He had realised she had started meaning something to him, something he didn't want to acknowledge.

But he had to stick to what he believed in. He could not give in to his grandmother's manipulative ways.

He had fixed himself a very strong coffee and headed up to take a very cold shower.

When Sara woke up and walked outside to the deck with her yoga mat, she was startled to find Zain sitting at the breakfast counter nursing a coffee. She didn't know that it was his third.

Rolling out her mat on the deck and trying to breathe in and out to calm her nerves, she was about to begin her routine when she heard more voices inside. Walking back in to see who it was so early in the morning, she found Zain hugging Saif.

'Sara!!' Saif got out of his brother's embrace and walked over to Sara. He gave her a warm hug and a huge smile.

'I am so glad to see you... how have you been? Are you going to do some yoga? Crap... I was hoping you could fix me a cup of that delicious *chai* and some breakfast.'

'I'll make you some coffee... let Sara do her yoga...' Zain quietly replied to Saif.

'No... no.. it's okay.. why don't you freshen up... I'll make us all some *chai* and breakfast...I can skip yoga today...' Sara smiled at Saif.

She busied herself in the kitchen, while Saif and Zain sat around the breakfast counter watching her.

'Saif, are you here at work?' Zain enquired.

'Yes, *bhai*, I have an interview with a firm here in New York. Dad must have told you that I wanted to work somewhere else, before I join you all in the business. I feel a little exposure will help me.'

'Yes, he did and I thought it was a wonderful idea... I did the same as well...' Zain patted his brother on his back and replied.

'Sorry to have landed up like this. I had messaged you, but found the message sitting in my outbox after I had landed this morning.' Saif was apologetic.

'Rubbish, you don't need to ask me for permission to stay here... Saif!' Zain brushed him off.

'I know...'

Sara smiled as she worked in the kitchen, listening in. It was wonderful to hear the brothers chat, she had loved the warmth and closeness the entire family shared with each other.

'Saif, did you come to New York from San Francisco or from somewhere else...?' Sara looked up from slicing the mushrooms and looked at Saif.

'Straight from home, Sara. Everyone sends their love.' he replied and turned to his brother and said, '*Bhai* the twins almost came with me. Thankfully Sana had a few meetings lined up... and Zoya is busy romancing her latest boyfriend...'

Zain smiled, 'Latest...? What happened... to the young architect Mum and Dad were made to meet a few months ago?'

Saif laughed, 'The young architect has been relegated to the underground basement of some building he was designing...'

'We now have a baker... who *Daadijaan* is calling a '*halwai*'...'

Sara started laughing, 'A *halwai*...? As in the kind who sits and makes sweets like they do in India... behind a counter rolling laddoos?'

Even Zain smiled at that description.

'No, no... he is a baker. Quite a well-known one, if I may say so. He runs a chain of artisanal bakeries... very posh... half Greek, so has all the female population ooh and awwwing over him... but, he seems to be interested in our Zoya... How only? God knows!'

Sara, placed mugs of steaming fragrant *chai* in front of both brothers and plates of scrambled eggs, sauteed mushrooms and buttered toast. She sat opposite them with her own food and joined in on all the gossip.

Sitting back and listening to Saif chat and watch Zain in this relaxed mood, filled Sara's heart. This was how it was supposed to be...

'Sara, *Daadijaan* wanted to know why you hadn't responded to her email with all the photographs of the party?' Saif asked her after a while.

Suddenly she felt Zain stiffen. His face lost the softness she had seen for the past ten minutes, it was as though someone had turned off a switch. Clearing away his plate of food and mug, he got up.

'I need to head to work. Saif, when do you need to go... and how long are you here for?' He spoke to his brother as he walked round the kitchen.

'I need to head out a bit myself, *bhai*... am here till tomorrow, I have a flight back in the afternoon. May I crash here... here in your study and uncomfortable couch?'

Raising his eyebrow at his brother's cheeky remark, Zain pointed out, 'Sara is in the study... you can camp upstairs with me.' saying this Zain left the two of them to finish their food and walked upstairs without a second glance or a thank you to Sara. Sara could feel him shutting himself away again.

Saif and Sara ate in silence for a few minutes.

'Sara, have you both not made up yet?'

'Made up? I don't know what you are talking about, Saif,' Sara spoke hesitantly.

Saif looked at her for a minute before he took out his phone, flicked something on and passed his phone to her.

'This...'

It was a picture of Zain, Sara, and Zorro at the sunrise place in San Francisco on *Daadijaan's* birthday.

Sara quietly stared at the photograph for a few minutes, gave a deep sigh and then passed the phone back to Saif.

'There is no 'this' Saif...' Sara's lips quivered as she replied.

'What do you mean? All of us felt it and saw it. The two of you had something on. Hell! We were hoping there was something on. I was sure there was something on...' Saif looked at her with a confused expression on his face.

'Why are you in the study? '

Sara looked at Saif, 'Where else should I be Saif... ?'

'Upstairs, in *bhai's* room! Come on Sara, don't think of us to be naïve and don't be a prude...' he shook his head in disbelief.

'Do you think we didn't know what was happening in SF...? And why should you hide it... you are his wife!!'

'Saif stop it!! I am not his wife!!!'

Saying this Sara walked away to the study leaving Saif sitting alone.

That afternoon, Sara received a message from Saif, apologising for their conversation in the morning. She replied that she forgave him and they must not talk about it anymore. She liked Saif and everyone else in Zain's family and didn't want to push them away.

After a lot of convincing and multiple messages, Saif convinced Sara to join him and a few of his friends for dinner that night. He had had a successful interview and mentioned that his brother had other plans.

Later that evening Sara found herself sitting in a crowded and noisy pub surrounded by Saif and a gang of his friends. They had all been in college together. They were now all working in New York and were meeting up because Saif was in town. She was being kept amused with all their stories, nibbling on some food that was placed in front of her and sipping on a liquid that tasted a little weird. Saif's friend, Alex, had ordered it for her saying she must try it. She was also politely inching a little away from the same friend who was trying to get a little over friendly.

'*Bhai*!!' Sara looked up when she heard Saif's voice, 'I am so glad you could join us. I was a little upset when you said you were busy.'

Zain was standing there in front of their rowdy table. He glanced at her for a minute.

Saying his hellos to the gang, whom he seemed to know, he declined a space to sit on the other side of the table and came around to where Sara was sitting with Alex.

He pulled a chair opposite them and smiled at the person next to him. Sara could feel his piercing gaze on her every now and then as he chatted with the person to his right. Sara was still trying to inch her way from Alex, who had draped his arm over the back of her seat.

'Alex... how have you been? Are you still working with James Everret?' Zain's deep voice stopped Alex in his tracks.

'Yes, Zain. I keep forgetting he is a friend of yours. Was he in school with you?' Alex stiffened.

'He was...'

Zain could see the relief in Sara's eyes, when Alex stopped moving closer to her.

'What are you drinking...?' Zain picked up Sara's glass and took a sip. He looked down at it and then looked at Sara.

'It is a good one... gives you a great buzz...' Alex chirped in leaning towards Sara.

Zain called the steward over, handed him Sara's glass and told him to throw it away.

'Bring me a single malt and a glass of merlot for the lady,' He turned to glare at Alex, 'Don't try these stunts again!' His voice came across as firm and stern.

Sara was horrified. What had she been drinking...?

'Hey... chill man!!' Alex turned to Sara and held up her hand and kissed her fingers, 'I didn't know you were a wine drinker,I could order you a bottle...'

'There is no need, she won't have more than a glass,' Zain growled, turning to Sara, he asked her if she was comfortable.

Sara looked relieved and said she would like to visit the restroom. She quietly slid out of the table area. Zain, stood up to let her move out, his arm brushing against hers and hands steadying her as she passed him.

Sara splashed her face with cold water in the crowded restroom. She tried to look at her face in the mirror in the middle of all the jostling among all the women inside. She had been relieved to see Zain step in and stop Alex's advances. She felt a sudden rush of hope and then pushed the thought aside. She had felt the same in the morning and then found Zain suddenly shut himself away again.

As she came out of the rest room, she found Alex waiting for her. Yikkees! She thought to herself. Alex grinned and took her hand and dragged her to the dance floor. Sara tried to stop him, but then found Saif and a few of the other girls there as well, so she smiled and joined them as they were dancing in a group. She was still uncomfortable with Alex dancing and swaying by her side, occasionally his hand straying and touching her on her arm and shoulder...

Zain was sitting nursing his drink at their table, chatting with some of the people there and occasionally looking out at some of their gang who had moved to the crowded dance floor. He had a clear view of them. He suddenly spotted Sara being led by Alex to the dance floor.

Sara was looking lovely. She was in a deep blue silk top and a pair of figure-hugging jeans. She had on her signature slim gold bangles on her wrists and delicate danglers on her ears, her eyes had their kohl and the rest of her face was the way she always kept it: clean and bare. He did spot a hint of naked gloss on her lips. Zain felt something stir inside him. He then also noticed Alex beginning to grope her in the pretext of dancing, Saif was close by but was distracted by all the other girls.

Zain got up, gritted his teeth and made his way towards the dance floor. The music had started to change to a slow number. Hell! There was no way he was going to let Alex dance with Sara.

Sara was trying to keep Alex's hands off her, when she suddenly felt a pair of strong and firm hands hold her by the waist from the back and span her midriff. She stiffened, but also felt relief.

'Thanks Alex... I will dance with Sara now.' A deep voice came out.

'Hey man! I am dancing with her, right Sara!!' Alex tried to be heard over the noise on the dance floor. The music had changed totally. It was now a soft one, with couples dancing slowly and moving to the beat of the music slowly very close to each other.

Sara turned to Alex and smiled at him, 'No, I am sorry Alex, but I think I would like to dance with Zain.'

As soon as she said this, she felt Zain move her to the other side, holding her close.

[25]

Suddenly Sara felt the world around her disappear. It was just them: Her and Zain.

He was holding her very close and she could feel every muscle of his body as they moved and swayed to the music. Zain moved his arms around Sara protecting her from the crush all around, moulding her body to his, drawing her arms around his neck, lowering his own arms down her back, holding her low around the hips. He felt it gave him a feeling of marking her as his own. She was in heels and so her face wasn't just at his shoulder, but a little higher tonight. Her eyes were level with his lips, his fingers were grazing her lower waist under the edge of her silk top. Her skin felt as soft as the silk she wore.

Zain looked down at Sara's head resting against his shoulder and moved his lips over her hair as they moved together.

Saif had asked him to join them to celebrate and he had politely declined. Then Saif had sent him a photograph of himself and Sara as they were leaving for the bar and also one of the entire group, standing outside the bar, waiting to enter. Zain's eyes were drawn to Sara standing next to Saif and also to Alex and another man looking down at Sara from behind. It hadn't taken him a minute to grab his coat and head out of his office.

Zain gently kissed her forehead. He had missed her. His mind had kept going back to their night together in his parents' house. It had been mind-blowing, and perfect, and then hell had broken loose after that. He automatically stiffened when he thought about how betrayed he had felt.

'*Bhai!*' Saif had come over to them, and without showing any surprise or raising an eyebrow, he continued to speak to his brother, 'We thought we would head to Jonathan's place for an after party... will the both of you join us?'

'No!' Zain's quick and curt reply did get a smirk as a reaction from Saif. Sara tried to hide under Zain's arm.

'O-kay!' Saif continued, 'Then I will see you both tomorrow for breakfast, around 10... is that alright and then head for the airport.'

Zain nodded at Saif and they watched him move back into the crowd.

The music changed and Sara whispered in Zain's ear that she could do with a glass of water. He followed her back to the bar and asked for a drink for both of them. Zain watched her move her head to the beat of the song being played, leaned in and asked, 'Did you enjoy yourself here at the club? It was something we all looked forward to when I was your age.'

Sara looked towards him and smiled, 'We did occasionally go to nightclubs when we were in college in Delhi, but not very often. Delhi wasn't always very safe at night. Plus, I sometimes find the music too loud. But, it was nice of Saif to invite me.'

Sara turned towards him and put her hand on his arm, 'Thank you for helping me out with Alex... I had a feeling there was something wrong with the drink he insisted I try and later as well.'

'Alex is a jerk... I will kill him when and if I see him again...' Zain shook his head, 'That drink was a sure shot lose your sense drink... you wouldn't have lasted long... anyway... he was acting like a teenager with hormones on overdrive.'

Sara tried to hide her smile at his description.

She turned back to watch people on the dance floor... while Zain continued to watch her. A few minutes later, she turned to him and said, 'I think I will go back now... you don't need to wait with me... I am sure Leyla is waiting for you...'

Sara climbed off the bar stool and headed towards the exit without turning back to look at Zain. Standing on the curb, trying to hail a cab to take her back to the apartment, she suddenly heard a deep voice behind her as a cab stopped right in front.

'Get in...' Startled, she followed his instructions, realising she really couldn't make a scene here on the street.

Zain shot off directions to the driver and sat back looking out of the window, his face a picture of grim concentration. Sara trembled sitting next to him... looking out of the other window.

Getting out of the cab, Sara tried to look for a way to escape, when she found a firm strong hand clutching hers and pulling her into the foyer of the building. They walked past Max, who perhaps sensed the tension and busied himself with his logbook. As soon as they entered the apartment and Zain shut the door, he pulled Sara into his arms and kissed her, holding her so close that she almost felt her bones crush.

Using all the force she had she wedged her arms between them and pushed with all her might..

'NO! No!...' Sara struggled to keep her own balance, after she managed to move Zain away... 'No! Zain!'

'Sara....?' He reached for her.

'No! Zain...I can't and I won't.... What do you think I am?' she held up her hands not letting him touch her.

'Sara...?' Zain just stood there looking at her.

'Do you think you can do whatever you want? One time you ignore me, then you seduce me... then... again you act as if I don't exist, then you accuse me of things... I don't even have any idea about... and now this...' Sara paused to take a breath.

'No... this is not happening!!!' She clenched her fists and glared at him.

Sara wrapped her arms around herself, she could feel herself trembling. She had to keep herself away from him. She knew she would melt and not be able to control herself if he touched her.

'Zain,I am here only for this week. I have a ticket for India on Sunday. Please let me stay till then. I will stay out of your way.' She walked a few steps and turned to him.

'I will have my father send you papers for the divorce. Once that comes through, we can then go our own ways... and forget about all of this... you will have won... and *Daadijaan* and as you say... I, her accomplice would have lost...' Sara said her piece and without even looking at Zain, she walked to the study and shut the door.

[26]

It had been a month since Sara had returned to India. She had spent time with her parents in Dehradun and had finally, after fielding questions from both parents and also her sisters, managed to sit her father down and tell him. She needed to meet a lawyer and they needed to sort out the divorce.

As expected, both her parents were stunned. They too had thought that her living with Zain would change things and finally bring them together. Her mother went on to add that they had heard fabulous accounts of her trip from not only *Daadijaan,* but also Zain's parents. Later when she was alone with her father, he had held her close and let her cry her heart out, without even probing further.

This was now her fifth week back. Sitting with her laptop in the garden, checking her email, Sara was surprised to receive an email from the MET in New York offering her a position on their team of curator trainees. She should have been thrilled, but Sara read and reread the email. This was an offer of a lifetime, but it would also mean going back to New York and living in the same city as Zain. Sara quietly shut her computer and sat nursing her mug of *chai.* She needed to think.

'That is an offer you shouldn't have to think twice about...' A deep voice spoke up right behind her making her almost spill the liquid inside her mug.

Sara swivelled around in her chair and with eyes as large and round as saucers and her mouth open... 'Zain!'

She had frozen at her spot. She hadn't expected him here in India, not in Dehradun, let alone in her father's house.

'Hi Sara, how are you?' Zain walked over to the chair opposite her and sat down, stretching his long legs out, his gaze never leaving her.

Sara was still stunned and didn't respond. Zain leaned in front, resting his elbows on his knees, he looked at Sara and repeated himself, 'How are you, Sara?'

'Why are you here, Zain?' Sara asked softly.

'I am here for some work,' Zain replied.

'Oh really? In Dehradun? I would have thought your work would have been either in Delhi or in Mumbai.'

'Delhi,' Zain replied. 'But, then I decided to come and see your father.'

'Why?'

'I thought your parents needed an explanation about us,'

'Zain? There is or was no us, you were very clear about it.' Sara's eyes flashed as she spat the words out.

'And, I think you're absolutely right.' Sara continued. 'There's no us. What happened in San Francisco was inevitable. It would happen between any two people who are forced to spend time together and are thrown at each other. That is what it was, nothing else.'

Sara realised her breathing had become patchy and her heart rate had increased in the due course of her speech.

She stood up, putting her mug of *chai* on the table in front of her, she started to walk inside to the house. As she passed Zain, he stopped her by holding on to her wrist.

'Sara, we need to talk...'

Yanking her hand out of his, 'No, we don't Zain! This isn't a game, and you are not the bully here. You cannot decide who plays the game and who does not. What happened all those years ago was a mistake, we were made into puppets by *Daadijaan* and no one really objected.'

Eyes flashing with anger, Sara continued, 'I am still to understand why none of our parents opposed it. None of our families are like the ones they show in Bollywood films, my father was not desperate to get my sister married and therefore had to oblige to *Daadijaan's* crazy terms... your father didn't need to agree either, why he did so, I don't know.'

'YOU!' her tone raised a notch higher than the rest of her speech, 'didn't need to either! You were an adult, educated and mature man, why did you agree? And, then you decided to leave the next morning and never turn back and ask what happened to the girl you 'married'. Doesn't that sound weird to you? Doesn't it reek of a typical Hindi film story...only sadly, it wasn't one. It was real life!'

She continued, 'I was too young, naïve, and stupid to ask these questions then, but I am not the same anymore. So now

I ask you, Zain, what game were you playing then and what game are you playing now?'

Sara's face was all flushed, she had never been so mad in her life. It was as though all the pent-up tension, anger and frustration was getting released all at one go. Sara glared at Zain and then turned around and ran inside.

Zain sat back in the chair and closed his eyes. He had spent the last month travelling all over the world to all their offices and had scheduled meeting after meeting into a packed schedule to keep himself busy and his mind diverted. He often took overnight flights so that he didn't have to spend a night alone in a room.

His parents and family had been calling him every day to speak to him, and he hardly ever took their calls, speaking only to his father about things related to work. He had become unbearable to spend time with. Thinking back, he felt sorry for his colleagues at work. He had stopped talking and only snapped.

All of that had ended only when he came home to his apartment one day to find Saif and *Daadijaan* sitting waiting for him. He had actually almost thrown them out, till finally he agreed to hear what they had to say. *Daadijaan* had acknowledged her own role in making the mess that she had created all those years ago. She apologised for her scheme and even begged him to forgive her.

Zain was still seething, when finally, Saif had walked over and then used all his might to sock him in the face. This had shocked both Zain and *Daadijaan*. When Zain glared at Saif, he yelled at Zain and told him he had enough of all the crap that was happening. He couldn't believe his older brother, his role model, was being such a fool and so ill mannered. He said he couldn't believe that Zain had been waiting for *Daadijaan* to apologize. Everyone knew what had been going on between Zain and Sara and it was ridiculous that instead of being together, he was disowning his feelings for her just because of his own pride. He had never seen such a fool.

Zain had drowned himself in alcohol that night, waking up the next morning feeling miserable, but with a clear head. He had been a fool, not just a fool, but the world's biggest idiot. Taking the next flight out of New York, he had landed in Delhi and then headed straight to Dehradun, when he was finally able to get Ashar to disclose her location. He wanted her back.

But hearing Sara speak and seeing the anger in her eyes, Zain realised he had messed up big time. She was right. He had blamed her uselessly, and had taken out all his anger with *Daadijaan* on her. He hadn't really thought about her all these years and even when he should have, he hadn't. He had spoken to Sara's father and apologised and told him his intentions. Her father had looked at him quietly for some time and then told him that he would not make the same mistake twice. Whatever Sara decided would have his support. He had then directed him towards the garden where Sara was sitting.

Zain stood up and went looking for Sara, he had to speak with her.

'Sara, please open the door, we need to talk!' Sara could hear Zain outside her door.

Silence... Zain knocked again- Silence...

He turned to find Sara's father standing next to him, 'Zain... she has made up her mind... I am sorry!'

[27]

Six months later....

Zain got off the phone, turned his chair to face the window behind him and looked out into the array of tall skyscrapers that made up Manhattan. Time had been crawling and despite immersing himself in work and being out with friends as often as he could manage, he felt a sense of blankness and numbness.

His eyes wandered towards the bottom drawer of his desk. Opening it, he saw the white envelope sitting quietly on top of some papers. He had received it two months ago, reading it, he had simply set it aside.

Picking up his phone, he checked her Facebook and Instagram profiles. There had been no updates in the past year. He had tried to find out from Ashar, even called Saniya once on some pretext to ask about Sara, but had received no reply. It was as though no one wanted to talk about her, or had decided to not tell him.

Zain was brought back to reality with the buzzing of his phone. Julie, his assistant, was calling to remind him of his flight to London.

Landing in London, Zain stepped out of the airport and was not surprised to find it raining and overcast. Upon reaching his usual hotel, he received a message that his meeting for the evening had been cancelled. He now had the entire afternoon and evening free.

Zain decided to grab a drink at a local pub nearby that he liked to frequent. Walking towards the pub, he passed the National Gallery and spotted huge banners publicising an exhibition of modern art. He stopped to read a banner and spotted a painting on one that he had seen on the cover of one of the thick books, Sara would be pouring over when she was at his apartment.

He didn't understand art too much, and preferred classical art and paintings that he understood. Some of the books Sara used to pour over had paintings that made no sense to him. Some had squares and some had some designs which used bold colours, but made no head or tail to him. What he was looking at was one of those, a large painting with boxes in bold colours. He remembered looking at it on the cover of a book and had glanced at Sara's two page analysis of it. He had been impressed. He had never thought of the painting from that perspective.

Checking his watch, Zain decided to go in and view the exhibition and then head to the pub. Stepping inside, Zain walked around amongst the crowds, he could hear people discussing the art work in hushed tones. Walking around looking for the painting he had spotted, he noticed a small crowd of school students all huddled in a cluster viewing a painting. As he walked closer, he heard a clear voice, explaining the painting and answering questions.

'Piet Mondrian was a Dutch artist and he was known for his abstract art.'

Zain had been startled to hear Sara's voice. He had no idea she was in London.

Sara turned to a student in front of her, 'What do you notice about this painting?'

'Lots of squares and rectangles...' replied the boy, 'It reminds me of Mrs Gray's geometry class...' groaned another.

'Ha Ha...! Very true, but did you know that Piet Mondrian never used a scale or a ruler to measure his lines and drew them free hand...' Sara went on smiling at the kids.

'My mum has a dress with a similar design...' whispered a little girl.

'Yes... a lot of Mondrian's work has found itself in clothes, upholstery and furniture...that is because the designs are eye-catching and the colours are bold. You surely have one fashionable mommy, Casey!' Sara winked at the little girl.

'How many of you like climbing trees?' She asked and beamed as soon as she saw many hands shooting up... 'Well! So did Mondrian and all his earlier paintings were about normal things and mostly trees...'

She led them to the next painting where she showed them one that resembled a tree, but asked them to look closer and spot the grid of lines, both vertical and horizontal ... to make the bark...

'It looks like he was practising drawing squares and lines...' piped up a girl pointing at the painting.

'You are absolutely right... Janice...' answered Sara glancing at the name tag pinned onto the little girl, 'Do you practise your sleeping and standing lines...? You could also paint like

Mondrian then....' And she guided her group along to the next painting.

Standing quietly to a side behind another group of people, Zain watched Sara interacting with the students. He could see the excitement on her face as she spoke to the kids. He had never seen her like this, no actually he had. She had the same expression on her face when the two of them had been together in San Francisco. He remembered her expression when she was viewing the Golden Gate bridge as well as the view from the hill near his parents' home.

Sara, felt someone watching her. Looking around she saw many eyes watching her as she interacted with the students, shaking her head as she tried to continue with her work. But, the tingling sensation continued. She took the group to the next painting and continued with her explanation. She'd been in London now for the past month. This assignment had been exactly what she had needed. It gave her an opportunity to get away from Dehradun and her family and took her to a new place where she could not think about Zain. She had been conducting these curated walks for students through the gallery for the past week and had been thoroughly enjoying herself. The students ranged from little ones to art students at times. Their questions and their awestruck faces fascinated her. She loved London, the vibe of the city reminded her of New York and this for her was the next best thing.

At six that evening, after finishing work and wrapping up her tasks, Sara wound her warm scarf around her shoulders and stepped out of the gallery and walked towards the small tea stall that was at the corner of the street. She had discovered it by chance. It was run by an old Indian couple from Haridwar. They made a variety of Indian teas, with cardamom, ginger and other spices. It was perfect in the cold and draughty London weather and had become a part of Sara's routine on her way home from work.

'Hello aunty! *Ek adrak chai,* please…'

'Make it two please,' a deep voice from behind her made Sara turn and she found herself standing in front of a broad chest. Raising her eyes, she followed the dark collar enclosed neck to the sharp jawline sporting a slight stubble and then onto the firm lips that slowly turned into a smile. Sara looked up into those dark eyes that she had been trying to forget.

She heard Zain speak, 'Thank you aunty!' he was reaching out for the two cups of piping hot tea. Sara watched Zain carry the two cups to the low wall near the stall where most people were standing sipping their *chai*. He put the cups down and looked towards her.

Swallowing slowly, she walked towards him, picked up her cup, leaned against the low wall so that she didn't have to look at him and said, 'Thank you.'

They sipped their hot *chai* in silence till, 'How are you, Sara?'

'How did you know I was here, who told you?' she quietly asked him.

'No one told me, no one… even when I asked, no one…' Zain replied in a low growl.

'Why?' Zain continued.

'How did you find me today?' Sara asked him a question instead, not wanting to answer his question.

'It was a coincidence....' Zain started to speak, when it started to rain suddenly. Both of them ran to take shelter under an awning nearby.

'I was heading to the pub down the street, will you please join me, Sara?' Zain asked her quietly in her ear. Sara felt a shiver down her neck and spine as Zain spoke, they were all huddled together with other people all trying to stay dry.

Gently nodding, Sara took out her umbrella and handed it to him to hold over both of them. They began to walk towards the old-style country pub in the middle of the bustling London district.

'How was it a coincidence, Zain?' Sara asked him after they had settled into a booth at the back of the pub.

Zain couldn't keep his eyes off her. The dim lighting and the yellow lamps and candles on the tables lit her face up in the softest glow he had seen.

'I spotted a painting by Mondrian, that I recognised from one of those thick books you used to keep at home, on a banner outside the Gallery..' He looked at her while he spoke, ' I had some free time so decided to go and see it properly. As I was walking around, I heard your voice. You are very good.'

'Good?' Sara asked, her eyes also not leaving his.

'Good at your work, I was quite fascinated with what you were telling those kids. They seemed hooked as well.' Zain replied.

'Since you are here, I want to know something. Why didn't you take the assignment at the MET?' he continued taking a sip of the drink the attendant had placed before him.

Sara licked her lips, taking her time to think of an appropriate answer. Zain clenched his fingers around his glass spotting this habit of hers that he loved. He had missed her so much.

'Should we order some food, I am quite hungry. Do you know what is good here? I cannot believe I hadn't spotted this place in the past month that I have been here.' Sara gushed trying to divert his attention.

Without moving his eyes off her, Zain signalled for the waiter to take their order.

'You have been in London for a month?' Zain asked.

'Yes, I got this assignment and it was too good an opportunity to miss. I get trained to curate as well as document, and I hadn't ever been to London. I like the city, the vibe is different and it reminds me of...' Sara broke off, realising she was going to mention New York.

'How are your parents?' Zain asked, looking at her. 'They let you stay here in London by yourself?'

'Yes, I am sharing an apartment with two other women, they are nice.' Sara replied.

Their food arrived and they began to eat.

'If there is one thing that I wish the British would learn is to add some spice to their food,' Zain said, sprinkling his food liberally with pepper and chilli flakes. 'We should have gone to an Indian restaurant.'

Sara smiled, remembering Zain eating the food she used to keep in the refrigerator and his thank you notes.

Suddenly, Zain put his fork down and held her hand, Sara looked puzzled. 'We need to talk!'

'But, we are talking...' Sara replied.

'No, we need to talk properly, not like this.' Zain signalled to the waiter to pack up their food and bring him the bill.

Sara looked at him confused.

He guided her outside. Thankfully it had stopped raining. Sara still looked at him confused. She saw him call for a Taxi, 'Zain, I cannot come with you... I am not going with you.'

Zain, ignored her protests, and pushed her into the taxi before him. Looking at the grim expression on his face, Sara decided it was best not to protest any further. She could always leave once they reached wherever they were going.

Sitting next to him in the Taxi, Sara was very aware of his thigh next to her, she tried to move away a little, but realised that he was still holding her hand, which he gripped tightly. She tried to release her hand, but his grip just became tighter.

Before she could protest any further, the Taxi came to a stop, they had reached wherever they were going. Zain got out and pulled her out with him as well. She realised they were in front of a hotel and she felt herself being ushered into the lobby, past the reception and into the elevator, her hand still in Zain's.

There were others in the elevator and she looked at Zain's face which was still and grim and then looked straight ahead.

Soon, Zain opened the door to a room and waited for her to enter. Taking a deep breath, Sara stepped into the room and found herself inside a nice big airy room, as she stood there just inside the room, she licked her lips and turned around and started to speak, 'Zain....' Before she could say anything else, she felt herself being pushed against the wall and Zain trapping her between the wall and himself.

His lips crushed hers, devouring them as though he couldn't have enough. Surprised by the suddenness of the kiss, Sara took some time to react. When she finally did realise what was happening, she tried to wedge her arms between them to protest, but Zain was too quick for her. He held both her wrists and moved them up around the back of his neck, bringing her closer to him, not once breaking the momentum of his kiss. Sara found herself responding to him, her own arms were draped across his shoulders and her hands were deeply entwined in his soft thick hair at his nape. She found herself pulling him down and closer as well, as though she didn't want to let him go.

After a while their kissing became softer and Zain lowered the intensity of his kiss, but still didn't let her lips go. His body was still wedged in between hers, grinding into her as he kissed her. He slowly let her lips go and moved his lips across her cheek to her right ear, nipping the skin, and showering tiny kisses as his lips made their way down her neck. He could feel the skin along her neck get heated as he licked and nipped. He could feel her hands still in his hair, he looked up to look at her face and saw her eyes closed and her lips parted.

He suddenly lifted her up and walked over to the bed. Lowering her gently, he sank into the bed beside her, drawing her close, hugging her with all his might.

'I missed you...' Zain whispered into her ear.

Sara's eyes flew open. What was happening? Panic spread across her face. This was exactly what she hadn't wanted.

This was what she had been trying to avoid. She knew that if she actually physically met him, she would have no way out.

Zain felt Sara stiffen, and instinctively pulled her closer. He saw her open her mouth to say something, most likely protest and immediately, silenced her with another soft kiss. Speaking into her lips, Zain whispered, 'I am not letting you go until you hear me out.'

He continued to kiss her gently, his tongue softly probing inside her mouth, his lips nipping around her lips, his leg nudging its way between her legs. Sara felt his hands moving gently down her neck towards her breast. He cupped her left breast through her silk top and grazed his finger across her nipple and she could feel her bud hardening at his touch. Zain moved his face down to her breast kissing her nipple, taking it into his mouth and sucking it through the silk, moving his hands further down across her stomach.

His hands gently slipped under the edge of her shirt, his fingers grazed against the waistband of her trousers, setting a trail of fire against her skin.

'It isn't fair!' Sara whispered not being able to control herself.

'What isn't?' Zain whispered, bringing his lips back to softly kiss the edge of her mouth.

'This...' Sara looked into Zain's eyes. 'You want me to hear you out, but I cannot... not while you do this...' Sara gasped as she felt Zain's hands move lower across abdomen and stop a few centimetres away from her core.

'Do you want me to stop?' Zain whispered into her mouth, as his hand cupped her core. Sara clutched Zain's shoulder, drawing him even closer.

'No, but if we have to talk then we will need to stop.' Sara replied.

Zain looked at Sara and slowly lifted himself off her. Sara suddenly felt a cold draft on her skin as soon as his warm body left hers. Zain stood up, raked his fingers through his hair not taking his eyes off her. He reached out and extended his hand to help her also get up.

Sara sat up and then asked quietly, 'Could I please just freshen up?' Zain nodded and pointed towards the washroom.

Ten minutes later, Sara emerged from the washroom, her face still slightly damp and her hair combed and in place.

Zain turned towards her holding two mugs of piping hot coffee. Sara looked at him.

'We shall both need this, if we want to talk, and I want to talk to you.' Zain said, looking at her straight. Taking her mug, Sara walked over to the couch that was near the window and sat down.

Zain followed her with his eyes. He was itching to take the mug from her hands and drag her back to the bed.

Sara looked towards Zain over the rim of her mug and said, 'Let's talk...'

Zain turned towards the window and looked out. He needed to sort this out, he couldn't mess it up. He took a deep breath and turned back towards Sara.

'I was an idiot.'

Sara looked at Zain, 'Sorry... I couldn't hear what you said...'

Zain looked at Sara straight without blinking an eyelid and said, 'I was an idiot, a fool… an egotistical fool!'

He walked over to Sara and sat down opposite her. Taking the mug of coffee out of her hands, he placed it on the table. Taking both her hands in his, Zain leaned forward.

'Sara, I was and am a fool. It took me too long, and finally a sock in my face from Saif, for me to realise what a selfish idiot I was being. I cannot believe I let my ego get between us. I didn't even stop to think about you and how you felt even once. I was so consumed by my anger with *Daadijaan* that I forgot about you.'

Sara took her hands out of Zain's and stood up. She walked towards the large window and looked out into the glittering view outside. She stood quietly and watched the lights across the Thames. Zain came and stood next to her.

Shoving his hands into his trouser pockets, he turned towards her and said, 'I want you… I need you. Please forgive me, Sara.'

Sara turned towards Zain to look at him while he spoke. 'I know I was angry about the *nikaah* and being forced into it. I was mad at *Daadijaan*, I shouldn't have blamed you. You were right about everything. I don't know why both our parents agreed to her hair brained idea… heck I don't know why I agreed… I really don't know what happened that night. You were not to blame at all.'

'It was my fault. I left the next morning refusing to accept what had happened. I wanted to get the wedding dissolved as soon as possible, but *Daadijaan* and *Baba* told me that we would need to wait for some time. I don't know why I agreed. I don't even know why I agreed to letting you stay with me when you came to New York. I don't know, Sara, why I agreed to anything, I have no answers.'

'I myself have been asking myself all these questions... and it is extremely frustrating. But, the truth is that I have realised I cannot live without you. I know I am being selfish and only thinking about myself and what I want, but am willing to try and hope that it is also what you want.' He paused to take a breath.

'I have had the worst time since I came to meet you, I know you might not agree, but I have. I tried to get in touch, but no one was willing to speak to me, or tell me anything about you. I have been living in total hell.' He continued slowly shaking his head.

Zain pulled his hands out of his pockets and held her and pulled her to him, 'I don't want to lose you now, but I know I need to give you time to make that decision yourself.'

Sara pulled herself away from Zain and moved away. Hugging herself, she nodded, 'Yes, I need some time Zain, I cannot decide quickly.'

She turned to pick up her bag and walked towards the door and stopped. 'How long are you in London?'

'How long do you need me to stay?' Zain asked quietly, looking straight at her.

'Please go back to New York, I don't know how long I will need.' Saying this Sara left the room.

[28]

Zain entered his apartment building as the sun was rising. He had just gotten off a long flight from Africa and was exhausted. He hadn't been home for two weeks and had been frightfully busy the entire time. There had been no call from Sara and he had promised to wait for her to decide. He owed her that much at least.

He walked towards the elevator and noticed that Max hadn't come on for his shift as yet. He smiled at the other concierge and pressed his key card to let him get access to his floor. Raking his hand through his hair, Zain realised he needed to sleep, but that had been something that had been eluding him. He realised he would need to do something about this soon; otherwise, he would be in trouble. Looking at his reflection in the elevator mirror, he realised he looked like a wreck.

The elevator finally pinged and Zain took a deep breath and walked into his apartment. As soon as he entered, he felt there was something different. Shaking his head, he told himself that it must be because he hadn't been home for so long. Yanking off his tie and leaving his bag by the door, he walked towards his living room. He could smell food, even a delicate fragrance of *chai*. Shaking his head again, he told himself he was hallucinating.

Zain wearily walked up the stairs to his bedroom, he needed to sleep and if he couldn't, he would take a shower and make himself some coffee and perhaps work. That seemed to be the only thing keeping him sane.

His room was all dark, he was about to walk over and turn on his bedside lamp when he realised something was different. The bed had been turned down and as his eyes focussed in the dark, he slowly saw a shape snuggled under the covers. It was a face he had been yearning to see. She looked angelic sleeping in his bed. Zain thought he was hallucinating. He sat down next to her on the bed and watched her as she slept. He couldn't believe it. Suddenly, he saw her open her eyes.

Sara opened her eyes and looked up straight into Zain's eyes. She had come in a few days ago and found the apartment empty. Max had let her in telling her that Zain hadn't been home in a few weeks. Sara had spent the past few days waiting for him, hoping her decision hadn't been the wrong one.

He looked tired. She could see the beginnings of dark circles beneath his eyes. She reached up to touch his face, tracing her fingers over his jawline and near his eyes.

Zain finally spoke, 'What took you so long?'

Sara placed her hand on his lips, 'Shhh... don't talk now. Come sleep, you need to sleep.'

She moved over to make space for him. Zain crawled into bed next to her, drawing her close against him, snuggling against her neck, he fell into a much-needed deep slumber.

It was almost dusk, when Sara opened her eyes. She had been sitting on her yoga mat meditating for some time. As she opened her eyes, she saw Zain sitting in front of her. She smiled at him and stood up, stretching as she did.

'*Chai?*'

As she walked past him towards the kitchen, he grabbed her hand and pulled her towards him, drawing her onto his lap, 'I cannot believe you are here, Sara.'

Sara smiled at him, 'Do you want me to leave?'

Zain looked at her in alarm. He quickly stood up carrying her inside with him, holding her very close. He sat down on the couch in his living room and kept her firmly on his lap. His eyes still locked with hers, he framed her face with his hands, bringing her face very close to his, he claimed her lips hungrily.

His hands slowly moved down her shoulders onto her breasts, cupping them and softly moulding them as he slid his hands lower. Sara's hands also reached for the edge of his T-shirt, yanking it up to remove it from over his head. He sat kissing her bare-chested, her hands roaming his chest and shoulders, grazing his nipples as her fingers spread over his chest. Zain gently pulled her T-shirt over her head and quickly snapped her bra off as well. He lifted her off his lap and tenderly lay her down on the couch, his hands sliding down her stomach and waist to the waistband of her yoga pants. Hitching his fingers inside, licking her enticing belly button and showering feathery nips around her waist, he tugged the pants off. As the cool air touched her skin, she could feel goosebumps covering her legs and arms. Zain quickly slipped off his tracks and covered her body with his. Lowering his mouth to her perked up nipples, he licked and sucked them, as Sara arched her back upwards, biting her lips as she felt dizzy with the sensations she was feeling.

'Zain, please…'

Sara's voice brought his attention back to her face, that was all flushed and hot.

'What? Zain, what?' Zain growled against her lips.

'Zain, please. I need you—now,' Sara whispered looking into his dark eyes.

Zain kissed her deeply, quickly moving her into a comfortable position, wedging himself in between her legs. Guiding himself to her core, he gently nudged her opening, finding it all wet and ready for him. Not removing his eyes from her, he pushed against her core and smoothly entered her, both of them arching with the sensation created with him sliding into her. Sara held on to Zain's shoulders and pulled him closer, wrapping her legs around his waist locking him in. She started to move against him, urging him on. Zain started moving gently at first, slowly moving in and out of her while he licked her neck.

'Faster, please!' Sara whispered, biting his earlobe, giving him the boost he needed to start increasing his momentum.

After a few minutes, he lifted her up with him and carried her upstairs to his bedroom. Gently depositing her on the bed, he crawled over her and whispered, 'I want to make love to my wife in my bed.'

Sara looked at him with a questioning look in her eyes.

Zain kissed her and whispered against her lips, 'Sara, I love you, will you be my wife?'

She looked at him, 'I love you too.'

Zain repeated, 'Will you be my wife, Sara?'

Sara felt him enter her once again, making her go over the edge again.

'Sara, tell me please, will you be my...'

'Yes, Zain I will...' Sara almost shouted out in ecstasy, hungrily reaching for his mouth.

She could feel him climaxing along with her.

A few hours later, Sara woke up to find herself entangled in sheets, covers and Zain's legs and arms. She turned towards him to find him awake watching her. His hands were gently rubbing her breasts. As soon as he realised she was awake, he leaned over and gently kissed her on her lips. She linked her arms over his shoulders and moved her fingers into his hair.

'Sara,' Zain's deep voice filled the room, 'Will you marry me?'

He propped up a beautiful diamond ring in front of her, holding her hand as he spoke.

Sara framed his face with her hands, 'Zain I am already married to you.'

'No, I want us to get married again—this time properly!'

'But, how can we get married a second time to each other, if we are already married?' Sara asked, looking puzzled.

'I will figure it out,' Zain said, slipping the ring onto her slender finger.

His phone buzzed right then. He swore under his breath, 'I am seriously going to throw that damn thing away!'

Sara giggled, slipping away from the bed, as he reached for his phone protesting at her moving away at the same time.

Sara walked into Zain's bathroom and slipped on his towelling robe. Tying the sash tightly around her waist, she walked down the stairs and straight to the kitchen. She needed her *chai*.

Brewing the milk and the cardamom with her tea leaves she stood in front of the hob, stirring the frothing milk, when she suddenly felt a pair of hands hug her from behind and a fuzzy chin nuzzle her neck.

Switching off the hob, she turned and pushed Zain away. Pouring the *chai* into two mugs, she handed him both and pointed towards the outside deck. She followed him outside with a plate of biscuits, which she explained, when she saw his bemused expression, she had bought from Mr Patel's store down the street. Sitting next to each other as they sipped their *chai*, Zain watched Sara dip her biscuits into her *chai* and then pop them into her mouth before they fell back into her mug. His lips curled into a smile when he saw her looking down at soggy biscuit bits in her mug.

'Let us get ready and go for a picnic in Central Park. I am not going to work today, so we can spend the whole day together.'

'Well, I have to stop by the MET around three in the afternoon. I have to sign my joining form,' Sara turned to Zain as she spoke. 'They got back to me before I reached London, I was going to move here, anyway. London was a short assignment.'

'So, you were going to move here anyway?' Zain looked at her and asked, raising his eyebrow.

'Yes…'

'Would you have told me?' asked Zain, moving closer to her and looking into her eyes.

'No,' Sara shook her head.

Zain pressed his lips together looking grim.

'You don't mind, do you?' Sara asked with a worried look on her face.

'Mind what?'

'As in, you don't have a problem with me taking up the assignment, do you?' Sara cleared her throat and explained.

Zain looked at her puzzled, 'Why would I object? Sara, please go ahead and do what your heart pleases. This assignment at the MET is very prestigious, I am very proud of you.'

'I just want you to know that I love you and support you in everything you do, like I hope you will too.' He continued.

Zain moved closer to her, lifting her onto his lap, enveloping her in his arms, 'I hope you will forgive me for being the terribly obstinate and headstrong person I have been.'

Sara reached up and kissed him gently. 'Shh! I love you too.'

'You had better, because I am never going to let you go, my dear wife!'

Acknowledgements

Unconsenting Adults was the first book I ever wrote. The idea had been tucked away in my computer for years, and during the COVID-19 lockdown, it took only a week to write. Interestingly, though it was my first, it is now being published as my third book.

After the back-to-back release of my first two books over two years, I suddenly found myself avoiding my favourite hobby. It took the encouragement, questions and occasional nudges from many people around me to bring this book to life, and I have them to thank as it finally finds its place in the world.

To begin with, I am grateful to my wonderful family, both immediate and extended. Their repeated questions, 'When is the next one out?' initially felt like pressure, but gradually became helpful reminders to get back to writing.

To my mother, who introduced me to romances without even realising it when I was in my teens. She would often roll her eyes at my so-called progressive romances, but kept reminding me, 'You told me there were six... where are the others?' Thank you, Maa, for your persistence and encouragement.

To my friend Gudrun, who was the first to read this story. She smiled, called it 'delicious', and reminded me to finish my sentences properly instead of relying so heavily on ellipses. Her feedback and enthusiasm were invaluable.

To my son, Joy, who helped shape the vision for the book cover, selected colour ideas, and gave the warmest hugs, which is something I now miss, with him living away from home.

To my daughter, Drishti, who has become my biggest fan. From sending me the funniest memes to cheering me on and telling me to write more, she has been a steady source of joy and motivation. She is the best giver of hugs and praise. My favourite sportsperson, my rockstar — I hope to base a character on her one day. I also hope she will read my books soon, and I do wonder why she hasn't already.

To my D, who never says no. Although I do not read his books, he continues to read, proof and offer advice on mine. Most of his suggestions are technical and often go over my head, but he has come to accept my usual one-word response: 'No.' I am grateful for his constant support and patience.

To my Facebook memories, which kept resurfacing with past posts, reviews and photos of my earlier books. They served as reminders that there was still one story left to finish.

To my friends and the kind readers who reached out asking about the other romances I had promised, thank you for your continued encouragement. You helped reignite my desire to return to storytelling.

To Samshad Huq Aunty, my mother-in-law's friend and my old neighbour, thank you for patiently answering my calls when I needed to check if I had written something correctly. Much of what I knew came from my love for Pakistani dramas, even though I was fully aware that Indian society had evolved in different ways.

To Zehra Abbas, who dismissed my hesitation with a raised eyebrow and said, 'Write what you want. Our society is very progressive among the kind of people your characters belong to. Don't worry.' That reassurance meant a lot.

To Jilani Bhathara at Indie Press, who gently followed up for two years, checking in to see if the book was ready and offering help whenever I needed it. Thank you for your patience. And a heartfelt thank you to the entire Indie Press team, especially my designer Sankhasubhro, who has designed all three of my book covers exactly the way I envisioned them.

This book will always hold a special place in my heart, as it was the very first one I wrote. I hope Unconsenting Adults receives the same warmth and love as my previous books did.

IndiePress

The best route your story can take.

To publish your own book, contact us.

We publish poetry collections, short story collections, novellas and novels.

contact@http://indiepress.in/

Instagram- indie_press